Swan Song

Swan Song

AN ODYSSEY

A novel

Lisa Alther

Alfred A. Knopf
New York · 2020

THIS IS A BORZOI BOOK
PUBLISHED BY ALFRED A. KNOPF

Copyright © 2020 by Lisa Alther

All rights reserved. Published in the United States by Alfred A. Knopf,
a division of Penguin Random House LLC, New York, and distributed
in Canada by Penguin Random House Canada Limited, Toronto.

www.aaknopf.com

Knopf, Borzoi Books, and the colophon are registered trademarks of
Penguin Random House LLC.

Grateful acknowledgment is made to the following
for permission to reprint previously published material:
Alfred A. Knopf: "Ithaca," "Remember, Body," and "Waiting for the
Barbarians" from *C. P. Cavafy: Collected Poems* by C. P. Cavafy, translated
by Daniel Mendelsohn, introduction, notes and commentary, and
translation copyright © 2009 by Daniel Mendelsohn. Reprinted by
permission of Alfred A. Knopf, an imprint of the Knopf Doubleday
Publishing Group, a division of Penguin Random House LLC.
All rights reserved.
Hal Leonard LLC: Lyric excerpt from "Angel Flying Too Close to
the Ground," words and music by Willie Nelson, copyright © 1978
Full Nelson Music, Inc. All rights administered by Sony/ATV Music
Publishing LLC. International copyright secured. All rights reserved.
Reprinted by permission of Hal Leonard LLC.
West Virginia University Press: "Swan Song" by Lisa Alther from
LGBTQ Fiction and Poetry from Appalachia, edited by Jeff Mann and
Julia Watts, copyright © 2019 by Lisa Alther. Reprinted by
permission of West Virginia University Press. All rights reserved.

Library of Congress Cataloging-in-Publication Data
Names: Alther, Lisa, author.
Title: Swan song: an odyssey / Lisa Alther.
Description: First edition. | New York: Alfred A. Knopf, 2020.
Identifiers: LCCN 2019022764 (print) | LCCN 2019022765 (ebook) |
ISBN 9780525657545 (hardcover) | ISBN 9780525657552 (ebook)
Subjects: GSAFD: Love stories.
Classification: LCC PS3551.L78 S93 2020 (print) |
LCC PS3551.L78 (ebook) | DDC 813/.54—dc23
LC record available at https://lccn.loc.gov/2019022764
LC ebook record available at https://lccn.loc.gov/2019022765

This is a work of fiction. Names, characters, places, and incidents
either are the product of the author's imagination or are used fictitiously.
Any resemblance to actual persons, living or dead, events, or locales is
entirely coincidental.

Jacket design by Jenny Carrow

Manufactured in the United States of America

First Edition

For Ina

The realisation of one's own death is the point at which one becomes adult.

—*Lawrence Durrell*

CONTENTS

Swan Song

Chapter 1

The Death Magnet

IT WAS SNOWING THE AFTERNOON JESSIE RECYCLED HER sex toys. A sharp wind from Canada was whipping sheets of white across the parking lot at the household waste dump in Burlington. It was like being smacked in the face by a line of wet laundry. Most Vermonters had the good sense to stay home during a blizzard.

Jessie hauled a black plastic bag from the rear seat of her CRV and emptied its contents into the garbage mangle. Driving home, she wondered if someone could trace this paraphernalia back to her via her tire tracks in the snow. She realized she had been watching too many episodes of *CSI*.

By abandoning this junk, was she acknowledging that her love life was now over? she mused as she exited from the interstate. Her conscious motive had been less terminal: Last week, while transferring names and numbers from her tattered address book onto her new iPhone, she had realized that many of her entries were now dead. She pictured herself dead and her son Anthony's finding her antique VHS tape of *Lesbian Hospital* while searching for her will. To spare him this trauma, she had decided to dispose of it herself.

Yet she had learned in therapy that unconscious motives were often at odds with conscious ones. Sadly, if you knew what your unconscious motives were, then they weren't unconscious any-more, so you could never claim to know them. But one of hers might have involved an interview with Jack Nicholson in a recent *National Enquirer* she had read in a Price Chopper checkout line. He had talked of realizing that it was no longer "dignified" for him to hit on young women in parking lots, as he was evidently accustomed to doing. Likewise, Jessie had recently stopped danc-ing at parties, feeling it was undignified for someone in early old age to do the Bump. But since when had either Jack or she worried about dignity?

Jessie dropped her keys into the pottery bowl on the chest in the entryway of her condo. She turned on the radio and plopped down in the leather armchair in her living room. Outside the French doors, circles of ice, like giant peppermint Life Savers, were forming on the surface of Lake Champlain. One midwin-ter day they would merge to form a solid sheet of ice. Before global warming, cars used to race up and down this ice. Skat-ers had twirled around it. Fishermen had sat drinking Bud in little wooden huts atop it. Iceboats had swept along it with sil-ver blades flashing and ghostly sails luffing. But now the ice was deemed hazardous. Last winter a pickup truck had broken through it and sunk. Jessie had signed the death certificate for its idiot driver in the ER.

Glancing around her living room, Jessie realized that she was completely surrounded by the ghosts of her ancestors in the form of their furniture, recently moved from her parents' house, the Victorian where she had grown up, which she had sold after her father's death. A sea chest bound with black metal bands had accompanied a family of flour millers across the Atlantic from

Ireland. A wooden shuttle had earned a living for some French Huguenot weavers from Picardy. A steepled clock on the mantel had kept time for a family of draft dodgers from the Saarland. Beside it sat an ebony jewelry box containing the ashes of Kat, her lover of twenty years.

"A cloud of witnesses," her mother used to call her ancestors. With the least encouragement she would quote the entire passage from the Book of Hebrews: "Wherefore seeing we also are compassed about with so great a cloud of witnesses, let us lay aside every weight, and the sin which doth so easily beset us, and let us run with patience the race that is set before us." Her mother had lived by these instructions. Her role model had been Laura Bush, who had sacrificed her own career as a librarian in order to advance that of her husband. But Jessie suspected that this cloud of implacable Protestants would probably view her as a laggard in the race of life—having long since abandoned organized religion, not opposed to the occasional sin, and rarely noted for her patience.

The snow outside the window had let up, but a stiff north wind was roiling the bay into swells that were surging against the ice-coated boulders along the shoreline. She reflected that if her love life wasn't, in fact, over, she had just made a big mistake. Or at least her parents would have seen it that way, since they never threw anything away. Her mother's favorite saying had been "Waste not, want not." On their anniversaries, her parents used to go to the Hallmark store in the mall. Each would pick out a card and hand it to the other. They would read them, replace them on the rack, and drive back home, pleased to have expressed the requisite sentiments to each other at no charge. Sometimes these spawn of the Great Depression went to the family waiting room at the hospital for the complimentary coffee.

At the cinema her father would retrieve a jumbo popcorn bucket from the trash can and present it at the counter for a free refill. They reused tea bags until they ran clear, turned old socks into vacuum cleaner bags, and refused to drain the bathtub in winter until the heat had dissipated throughout the upstairs.

Yet their profligate daughter had just discarded a still-functional vibrator. But you could hardly donate it to Goodwill for a tax deduction, or pass it down as an heirloom. Though, according to the *Enquirer,* a family in Bar Harbor, Maine, had recently found hidden in a nook of their ancestral manse an ivory dildo, scrimshawed with couples locked in exotic embraces. The family concluded it had belonged to a great-grandmother, the wife of a whaling ship captain, whose voyages had lasted for two years at a time.

Why is it so unnerving to imagine a great-grandmother with a dildo? Jessie asked herself. She knew firsthand that the hungers of the flesh didn't flag with the years, even though the energy and opportunity to fulfill them might. But younger people preferred to imagine that they had invented sex. Like Facebook, once they discovered that their parents did it, too, it lost some of its allure.

An old gray mare behaving like a colt was perhaps distasteful to some. But Jessie's memories of her colt days in Vermont in the 1970s remained vivid. She had belonged to the Multiple Relationship Group, which had insisted that monogamy was a male invention designed to enslave women. The members were expected to conduct as many simultaneous affairs as possible. Their meetings were spent dealing with the resulting rage and misery, archaic emotions, the group agreed, that women were conditioned to express by a patriarchy intent on keeping them in chains.

From the radio came the voice of Celine Dion, wailing the theme from *Titanic*. As Celine explored the erotics of drowning in an icy sea for want of a life raft, Jessie felt suddenly bereft. Love and its loss used to incite in her a turmoil similar to Celine's. But now that Kat had died, Jessie couldn't imagine loving ever again. Humans were the only species that based their happiness on relationships that both partners knew would inevitably end in grief for one or the other.

Jessie turned off the radio and climbed the steps to her bedroom, passing artwork Kat had collected on trips abroad to promote her books—a Samoan tapa cloth, an Aboriginal dot painting, a Chinese pen-and-ink drawing of a waterfall, an oil painting in tones of gray and blue of the English town in which Virginia Woolf had spent her childhood summers. Upstairs, some unread medical journals lay on her desk. She eyed them warily. New research used to excite her, too. As a resident at Roosevelt Hospital in New York City, she had believed she and her colleagues would transform this wounded world into a place of compassion and healing. The world had rung its changes on them instead. What difference had their long hours of service made? The ice caps were still melting. Terrorists were still murdering hapless civilians. Ebola was on track to become a new Black Death. Sooner or later what now passed for Western civilization would collapse. The overheated Earth would ignite into an inferno. Billionaires would flee to other planets in their spaceships. Chaos would rule the streets, and gargoyles leering down from Gothic drainpipes would howl their triumph in the piercing rays from an angry red sun.

Jessie stretched out on her bed and reached for Kat's final journal, a lined school composition book with a black-and-white mottled cover. Jessie had found a dozen of them among Kat's papers, one for each of her published books. There was no apparent organization to them. Recipes and grocery lists mixed with quotes from whatever books she had been reading. She had also written out entire poems by others, along with drafts of new poems of her own. She had recorded overheard conversations and sketches of characters who were evolving in her imagination. She had pasted newspaper clippings and printed-out e-mails on the pages. It was a stream-of-consciousness screenshot of Kat's busy brain as she generated her next novel.

In the first eleven journals Jessie had been able to watch this chaos condense into finished books—like the clouds of matter from the Big Bang congealing into stars. After college in Boston, Kat had moved to a commune in Vermont, where she grew vegetables, raised livestock, made cheese, wove cloth, married, and gave birth to two sons, Martin and Malcolm. Her commune had fabricated giant puppets of political figures, which they had paraded in anti–Vietnam War demonstrations all over the country. She wrote a satirical novel about those years, which became a bestseller. She published several more novels, taught and did readings, and wrote articles for newspapers and magazines, cobbling together a living for herself and her sons after her marriage ended. But the story that had been brewing as Kat was dying had remained unwritten. By studying the twelfth journal, Jessie was hoping to discover what had been on Kat's mind during her final agonizing months.

On the first page Kat had written out the poem she had later asked Jessie to recite at her memorial service—"Ithaca," by Constantine Cavafy. Jessie had done so in the Interfaith Chapel on the shores of Lake Champlain, with sunlight pouring through the skylights onto the ebony jewelry box in which Kat's ashes reposed:

> *As you set out on the way to Ithaca*
> *hope that the road is a long one,*
> *filled with adventures, filled with discoveries. . . .*

Jessie glanced out the glass doors beside her bed. A frail winter sun was emerging from the storm clouds to begin its descent toward the snowy peaks of the Adirondacks on the far side of the lake. Abruptly she realized that a dark blob was floating in the water at the foot of the bank on which her condo perched. As she studied the blob, it dawned on her that it was clad in blue jeans and a forest green parka. It lay facedown, arms and legs splayed like a starfish. The swells were slamming this body against the rocks and then dragging it back out to open water.

After phoning 911, Jessie raced downstairs, pulled on her parka and boots, and ran out to the bank. The body was bobbing in the surging water. Copper-colored hair drifted around the head like the skeins of spun gold in "Rumpelstiltskin," which she had read to her granddaughter the previous evening. Hearing the cacophonous sirens of the ambulance, fire truck, and police cruisers as they wove through the streets of her neighborhood, she resisted the impulse to clamber down the cliff and probably break her neck. Soon blue and red lights were flashing in the gloom of the glowering sky.

She recognized one of the policewomen. Back in the day, Brenda and she had belonged to a women's karate group. A surgeon at the medical center used to drape his arm around Jessie and grope her breast as they emerged from the OR. She repeat-

edly asked him to stop, but he wouldn't. Finally she got skilled
enough at karate simply to throw him to the floor. While he lay
there cursing on the tiles, she just stepped over him and walked
away. He never touched her again.

In her off hours, Brenda taught a gun-safety class at a local
firing range. Jessie and Kat had taken the class when Kat bought
a handgun to store in her Subaru after some drug thug keyed
her car while she was researching a piece for the *Free Press* on the
opioid crisis in Vermont. This crisis heralded a seismic shift from
Vermont's commune days, when both Kat and Jessie had come
of age. Drugs then had concerned the search, however loopy, for
personal peace and a higher purpose. Now it involved profits for
the Bloods and Crips and Latin Kings.

During the gun class, Brenda revealed that she had Glocks
stashed all over her house so that one would always be available
no matter where an intruder might break in. She taught their
class to yell "GET OUT OF MY SPACE! I HAVE A GUN!"
Whenever Kat had been in a bad mood, she had yelled that at
Jessie.

Brenda nodded to Jessie as she and several other cops and
EMTs climbed down the bank. Two in hip boots waded into the
water and pulled the rigid corpse to shore. A medic felt for a
pulse at the neck.

Even from the top of the bank, Jessie could see that the woman's face was contused and lacerated. They zipped her into a black
body bag and loaded it on a stretcher, which they passed from
hand to hand up the cliff. Placing the stretcher on a gurney, they
rolled it across the condo lawn. Some neighbors, gathered on the
sidewalk, watched in appalled silence.

As another cop stretched yellow crime-scene tape around the
beach and bank, Brenda questioned Jessie. It was a short inter-

view, since Jessie had nothing to tell, apart from her spotting of the body in the water.

"Do you think someone killed her?" asked Jessie.

"Too soon to tell. Just keep your sidearm nearby, like I taught you."

JESSIE SANK BACK DOWN IN HER LEATHER CHAIR AND TRIED to recall where her sidearm was. She had probably left it in its hiding place in Kat's Subaru, which they had sold after Kat's Barrett's esophagus had morphed into esophageal cancer. Murder, suicide, or an accident? The woman's face was battered, but that might have resulted from falling off a cliff or being pounded on rocks by the waves.

A recent FBI sting had identified a major route for both the drug trade and sex trafficking that ran from Montreal, across the densely forested New York border, down the interstate on the far side of the lake, to New York City. Kat had written her final article on it. Overdoses had been skyrocketing at the Burlington ER. Jessie had dealt with one every few days. The woman in the lake looked eastern European. Could she have died trying to escape from traffickers? The ferries to New York State were still running. Could she have jumped off one and been carried south by the currents?

Jessie realized her imagination was in overdrive again. But she had seen so much grim stuff working in the ER, and had heard so much from Kat, that she knew anything was now possible in Vermont. As children, she and her two brothers had mocked their father, calling him "Dr. Death." Because of his months in French field hospitals during World War II, and his stints at Roosevelt Hospital in New York and at the Burlington medical center afterward, he had been convinced that if his children water-skied, they would collide with a dock. If they rode horses, they'd be thrown and become paralyzed. But over the years she had learned that disaster really did lurk around every corner. So much of his unbearably anxious behavior had made sense once she became a parent to Anthony and Cady. He had been trying to protect his children. She got that. She had apologized to him on his deathbed for her years of impatient scorn. He said he hadn't noticed.

This beautiful lake out her window—140 miles long, 15 miles across, 400 feet deep in spots—was a joy in the summer, when the surface was glassy and sunstruck. But during other seasons, this same lake could turn terrifying. As was happening at that very moment, a sudden blast of north wind could whip up ocean-size breakers that eroded banks and swamped boats at their moorings.

During her childhood she had been entranced by these fickle moods. She and her older brothers, Stephen and Caleb, had motored around the lake in a Boston Whaler in all kinds of weather, in and out of inlets, on and off other people's islands, in those halcyon days before children were required to phone their parents every five minutes to assure them that they hadn't yet been kidnapped. They had laughed wildly into the wind as they rode the breakers in their trusty Whaler, dodging stabs of lightning. It was a wonder they had lived to reach adulthood.

She remembered sitting in this living room, watching on TV as the twin towers imploded. She had sat paralyzed for a long time while footage of the planes crashing into the buildings replayed repeatedly. Eventually she had shifted her gaze out the French doors to the turbulent lake and had spotted an unmanned sailboat drifting past, mast snapped and hanging double, riggings snarled, tattered sail flapping as the boat bucked the crashing waves. Soon the overcast sky above the lake had filled with jets scrambled from the Plattsburgh air base, heading too late to New York City, their deafening roar bouncing back and forth between the Adirondacks and the Green Mountains.

Jessie was old enough now to recognize that world crises came and went in perpetually recurring cycles. Several years before she was born, her father had gone to war against the Germans. But he eventually came back home. Then the Cold War heated up, and she and her classmates had hidden from atom bombs beneath their desks at school. Some boys she knew in high school had been drafted to fight communism in Vietnam. A few returned in body bags, or with missing limbs. Her brother Stephen had served there as a medic and still woke up screaming from nightmares.

But later the Berlin Wall came down, and strangers embraced on the pedestrian mall in Burlington, just as they had in Times Square on V-E Day. It appeared for a time as though the perennial dream of a world at peace might now be possible. The funds squandered to defend against marauding Nazis and stealthy Communists could instead be used to feed and house, heal and educate people all over the globe. But those collapsing twin towers had derailed this reverie, and now the West was once again bankrupting itself in a struggle against sinister foes who kept popping up in new places and fresh disguises, like an endless game of Whac-A-Mole.

Reviewing her thoughts, Jessie diagnosed herself as suffering from PTSD. She would be minding her own business when, out of the blue, an image of Kat or one of her parents as they lay dying would assail her. When you started seeing only the sadness of life, with none of the simultaneous beauty and humor, you were in trouble. Her mother, her father, and her lover had all died within the past two years. It was one thing to tend patients, but something else again to watch your own loved ones shrivel up like dried apples. By dealing with death so closely for so long, had she become a death magnet? Mysterious corpses were now floating right up to her doorstep.

Chapter 2

Arabian Nights

JESSIE SAT BEHIND THE ADMISSIONS DESK IN THE *AMPHI-trite*'s clinic, writing an e-mail on her MacBook Air, trying to explain to Anthony and Cady, and to Malcolm and Martin, her abrupt departure from Burlington to accept this position as a physician on a cruise ship. She was careful not to mention the fact that she didn't want to spend her twilight years baby-sitting their children. She knew some grandmothers who refused to baby-sit. The less forthright ones simply moved to Boca Raton.

The engines were vibrating beneath her like a cat purring. It was hypnotic. But she needed to stay alert because cases of noro-virus were popping up all over the ship. The sea was rough, and waves were sweeping up over the portholes, making her feel as though she were trapped inside a sloshing aquarium.

A new e-mail from Brenda appeared on her screen, informing her that the investigation into the death of the woman in the lake had been closed. They had found her shoes and purse on a rock ledge not far from Jessie's condo. The purse still contained cash and credit cards, ruling out a robbery. The woman had lived in Burlington's North End, and her friends said she just liked to wade in the lake. The autopsy showed no trace of drugs or alcohol. A head injury had killed her. It was possible someone had pushed her off the cliff, but there was no suspect or motive. It was down to suicide or an accident, most likely an accident, since no note had been found and no depressive symptoms had been noticed by her friends or family.

Jessie shrugged irritably. As a physician, she had been trained to locate causes and effect cures. Unsolved mysteries annoyed her. It still seemed weird that the woman would have chosen to wade in a lake full of ice.

The phone rang several times. Since Amy, the nurse practitioner on desk duty, didn't answer, Jessie did. A man in suite 10024 reported that he was vomiting and had diarrhea. Jessie told him she would stop by his room right away for a stool sample. He laughed and said he didn't know that doctors made house calls anymore, much less in the middle of the Arabian Sea.

As Jessie headed for the service elevator in her white slacks and epauletted uniform shirt, with her lavender stethoscope draped around her neck like unattractive tribal jewelry, she reflected that norovirus wasn't something to joke about. Hand-sanitizer dispensers had been set up all around the ship, with signs urging people to use them. If they couldn't short-circuit this outbreak, the buffets and pools might have to be shuttered. The ship would need to divert to the nearest port to be disinfected. It could cost the cruise line millions and ruin the holidays of the passengers, some of whom had saved up a lifetime for this trip.

And most important to Jessie, this would leave her unemployed, with too much free time in which to remember how it had felt to close her mother's eyelids with her fingertips:

The lids popped back open, and the hollow amber irises, flecked with gold and russet and copper, seemed to gaze right past Jessie toward the sunlight streaming through the window. Jessie closed the lids again. Again they flipped open. Her mother looked as startled as Jessie felt. This was why the Greeks had weighted down the eyelids of the dead with coins.

Jessie held the lids shut for a long time. She removed her fingers carefully, as though performing a magic trick. The lids remained closed. Straightening up, she stepped back from the narrow bed. At her mother's request, Jessie had moved this bed from her parents' house to the rehab center. Her mother's spinster aunt Emma, for whom her mother had been named, had slept in it for most of her life. And now her namesake had died in it.

Jessie's mother was lying atop a Double Wedding Ring quilt her own grandmother had pieced. The wedding rings in question resembled the neck shackles worn by slaves. Her mother was dressed in the blue slacks and yellow golf shirt Jessie had bought for her stay in this facility following her heart attack. Everyone, her cardiologist included, had assumed that she would soon be back home again. She was also wearing the white Velcro-strapped tennis shoes Jessie had bought her. Jessie realized how mortified her mother would be to know that she was lying on this ancestral quilt with shoes on, so she slipped them off and set them in the closet. She felt absurdly pleased that her mother had chosen this outfit in which to die. Traditionally, she had returned any new clothing Jessie bought her for a refund, preferring to wear hand-me-downs from Jessie and Kat. Kat was quite tall, and Jessie quite short, like Mutt and Jeff from the Sunday comics of long ago. So none of their castoffs really fit her mother, but at least they were free.

The nurses had withdrawn. Jessie knew she had a few minutes before the house physician arrived to issue the death certificate and the funeral home came to collect the body. She sat down beside the bed and took her mother's hand in her own. It was already turning cool. Jessie was a *hardened physician who had dissected corpses in medical school and done innumerable autopsies since. She had watched many patients die, so she was taken aback to discover that tears were bathing her cheeks and dripping onto her mother's new yellow golf shirt.*

THE MAN WHO ANSWERED THE DOOR OF STATEROOM 10024, Charles Savage, was silver-haired, with a part so precise that it could have been sculpted by a razor. His erect bearing, apparent even in his white terry-cloth guest bathrobe, suggested a military background. His much younger wife, Gail, was statuesque, with a blond ponytail and eyes as turquoise as an Antarctic crevasse. She had the looks of a beauty queen turned trophy wife.

While Charles was in the bathroom providing a stool sample, Gail, attired in a sage green silk dressing gown, prowled the room like a caged tigress, sitting on the couch, standing up, circling the glass-topped coffee table, perching on the edge of the king-size bed. She slid open the glass door to the balcony and then closed it again. She kept sipping a brown liquid from a cut-glass tumbler. Jessie could smell alcohol. She could also detect a hint of Samsara perfume, which she recognized because Kat used to wear it, too. Jessie associated that scent with some of her happiest moments—collecting a stool sample from a stranger not among them.

At medical school, one of the first challenges had been to conquer the normal animal reflex of revulsion at the sight and smell of bodily fluids—blood, semen, saliva, pus, mucus, feces, urine, vomit. These were the tools of the medical trade, and their analyses were crucial to a diagnosis. Some students couldn't face it and had to find other careers. Blood had especially appalled

Jessie, and she had experienced shudders of physical pain when viewing other people's gory wounds. But repeated exposure eventually cured her of these unhelpful responses.

Her father's father had been a doctor in a small Vermont farming town, trained near the turn of the twentieth century at the University of Vermont's College of Medicine in Burlington. He had volunteered to join an American medical unit that went to France during World War I to work at the American Hospital near Paris. While there, he met and romanced Jessie's grandmother, the only woman surgeon at a nearby hospital in the Lycée Pasteur.

Her grandmother had grown up in New York City and was one of the first women to serve as an ambulance surgeon, riding into slums under a police escort. She had once treated a dozen partygoers who had acquired tetanus from injecting heroin cut on a dusty mantel. Upon returning from France, she had marched in the suffrage parades in Washington, D.C., and New York City, with swarms of hostile men jeering from the sidewalks. When women finally got the vote, she had said how pleased she was no longer to be classified with prisoners, children, and the insane. How Jessie's grandfather had persuaded her to move to the Green Mountains was a mystery. She must have really loved him. They practiced together, she driving a converted hearse into the little mountain towns for impromptu clinics, he riding a horse where their ambulance couldn't go.

Jessie remembered as a small child watching her grandfather observe a patient crossing his office floor to his desk. Before the patient could sit, her grandfather had announced, "Pneumonia." An X-ray at the Burlington hospital confirmed this diagnosis. This intuition both her grandparents had possessed still seemed like magic to Jessie. She and her medical peers, lacking such self-confidence, honed by decades of experience, relied instead on MRIs, CT scans, PET scans, blood tests, and X-rays. Of course her grandparents hadn't been traumatized by the threat of multimillion-dollar lawsuits if they made a mistake. In their day, patients had been grateful when doctors could help them, rather than litigious when they couldn't.

Later that night, after a test by Stan—the lab technician from Glasgow—had confirmed norovirus, Jessie returned to suite 10024 with a box of latex gloves and a bottle of hand sanitizer. She explained to Gail the need to use them as she cared for her husband, and the importance of washing her hands often, for as long as it took to sing "Happy Birthday." She assured them that a nurse would return twice a day to check on Charles's progress, and she instructed them to remain in their cabin until she released them from quarantine. They could order their meals from room service. A steward specially trained to deal with the virus would deliver them and would clean their cabin.

"Are you telling me that I can't leave this suite that we've paid tens of thousands of dollars for?" asked Gail.

"I'm sorry, Mrs. Savage, but that's exactly what I'm telling you."

"But *I'm* not sick!"

"We don't know that. We need to keep you isolated until the incubation period has passed. We can't risk your infecting other passengers."

"But one of them must have infected Charles in the first place."

"True. But it's not as though you can identify that person and take revenge. He or she is probably already well again."

Gail heaved a long-suffering sigh.

———

AS THE CABIN DOOR SUCKED SHUT BEHIND THE DOCTOR, Gail threw off her robe, revealing a black lace bra and thong. She rifled through her closet.

"What are you doing?" called Charles from the bed.

"If that little old lady thinks she's going to ruin my cruise, she's got another think coming." Gail pulled on an embroidered emerald green galabiya she had bought during the previous year's trip to Egypt. "Tonight is the Arabian Nights Gala, and I'm certainly not going to miss it."

"But you heard the doctor, Gail. You're supposed to stay here. You could spread the virus to other passengers."

"If I'm sick, I'm sick, thanks to you. If other passengers get sick from me, that's their problem."

Charles watched her wrap her blond hair into a French twist and secure it with a tortoiseshell clasp. Then she applied plum lipstick and smoky gray eye shadow in the mirror on the closet door.

As she swept into the hallway in a cloud of Samsara, Charles felt like weeping. They had been so much in love when she had been a nanny to his children. The split with his wife to marry her had been catastrophic, both emotionally and financially. But it had seemed worth it because, at age eighteen, Gail had been thrilled to be the wife of a World War II veteran, a boatswain's mate decorated for valor after Okinawa. His first wife and many friends had warned him about May–December romances, but he had ignored them. It was true that he rarely managed to satisfy her sexually anymore, and he wasn't supposed to take ED medications because of his heart condition. Nonetheless, he had brought along some Viagra just to try it out. He had also been considering an implant, but what was the point if Gail didn't even want him? This cruise was supposed to be a second honeymoon that would reignite their passion, but Gail left him behind in the cabin every chance she got.

Still, it was wonderful to be back at sea again. Several other men from his World War II battleship had also arranged to be on board with their wives. They planned to visit the battlefields of El Alamein once the ship reached Alexandria. Meanwhile, they had been meeting every afternoon to play Texas hold 'em on the pool deck, just as they had done all those years ago in the North Pacific. They wore royal blue baseball caps one of them had brought, printed on the front with the words NAVAL VETERAN and an insignia involving an anchor wrapped with chains. It was such a relief to relive those terrifying episodes off Okinawa with others who had shared them.

JESSIE LOCKED UP THE CLINIC AND RETURNED TO HER cabin in the staff quarters on the eleventh deck. It felt tiny compared to Charles and Gail's suite, and it had just a large window rather than French doors leading to a balcony. But she preferred to regard it as cozy rather than cramped. Also, since a steward would clean it, change her sheets, and do her washing every week, it felt to her like the Plaza. She removed and hung up her white uniform, donned the happy-face pajamas Kat had given her, and climbed into her bed.

Having departed from Sri Lanka that morning, the *Amphitrite* was currently crossing the Arabian Sea en route to Dubai. The nurses had described Dubai as a pearl-diving village that had recently transformed itself into a space-age metropolis—a Disneyland of the Arabian Desert.

She was a long way from Burlington. This had been her intention when she signed the six-week contract (which Ben, the lead medical officer, said would be extendable once they reached Brooklyn). She had been the porter at death's doorway for too long. Vermonters were peaceful people compared to most Americans, comprising the highest per capita population of Buddhists of any state. But when they weren't meditating, they sometimes ended up in her ER. Her confidence in human kindness and common sense had been undermined over the years by the steady flow of knife and gunshot wounds, battered women, rape victims, and drunks and druggies who had wrecked cars, motorcycles, ATVs, motorboats, Jet Skis, and snowmobiles. When she was younger, she had been proud to regard herself as a kung fu warrior, poised to defeat whatever accident or disease burst through the door of her ER next. But after her parents and Kat became ill, she had been forced to face the fact that there were some opponents she couldn't outwit or overpower.

Once they were gone, she took a leave of absence from the ER to clean out and sell her childhood home on a hill overlooking the Burlington harbor. She attended endless meetings with lawyers and accountants and wrote checks to the IRS, the state of Vermont, and her brothers. Although the youngest sibling, she was the only one still living in Vermont, so she had been tasked with the thankless jobs of final caregiver and executor for her parents.

Her mother left a mountain of shoe boxes crammed with every piece of paper any member of her family had ever touched since the middle of the nineteenth century. Jessie posted the photos and genealogical charts on Ancestry.com and organized the letters by author and date. She had no idea why she was doing this, since the younger generations of her family weren't remotely interested, but she wasn't going to be the one to jettison these relics. Her children could throw them all away once she died, because they wouldn't feel any guilt.

Jessie's father had left several dozen black plastic garbage bags crammed with junk mail. She had had to sort through it all because here and there among sweepstakes mailings and charity solicitations a stock certificate or insurance policy would surface. She had even found two loose diamonds of unknown origin. She had also found bottles of expired painkillers stashed all around his office and bedroom. Dilaudid seemed to have been his favorite.

As for Kat's detritus, her drafts, manuscripts, reviews, and publicity materials filled two dozen plastic bins at one end of their garage. Jessie assumed they should go to a university library somewhere, but she hadn't dealt with that yet. She was interested only in those journals. She had brought the final one with her on this voyage, determined to understand how such apparent mayhem could yield a finished book with a coherent plot and recognizable characters. She also needed to know what Kat had been thinking as she faced her own death.

Once the dust clouds from her loved ones' deaths had settled, Jessie had faced the decision of what to do with herself next. She was eligible for Social Security, and she had an adequate 401(k). But her father had worked until he was seventy. He had said he knew it was time to retire when laparoscopic surgery came in and he had lacked the interest to retrain. But she dreaded all the free time retirement would allow. She had always avoided distressing topics like the meaning of life by being too busy to think about them. That had been Kat's department. In earlier eras, useless old women had been burned as witches. If you couldn't produce babies, no longer titillated men sexually, possessed money and property others coveted, you had to go. That body in the lake, floating right up to her deck, had been merely the last straw in an entire bale of despair.

But then Jessie had received an e-mail from Ben Armstrong, who had been a resident with her at Roosevelt Hospital in New York City. They had had a brief, uninspired affair and had occasionally run into each other at conferences since. Ben was in charge of the clinic on a British cruise ship called the *Amphitrite.* His second-in-command had had to cancel at the last moment because of illness. From college courses, she knew that Amphitrite was Poseidon's wife, Queen of the Seas. A ship named for such a powerful goddess had seemed a positive omen. So Jessie had embraced this chance to sail through Southeast Asia and the Middle East on her and had boarded a flight to Hong Kong a few days later. She was now serving her patients on board as well as she could, but then they would disembark and go back home to their own physicians. A new set of potential patients would board, and she would never have to see the previous ones again, much less help them die.

The shadow side of such transience, though, was isolation. Ben, the four nurses, and the lab tech, as well as the rest of the staff and crew, were friendly but distant. Quarters were close, and contracts for permanent staff were long. It was important to guard your privacy. Late at night in the belly of the ship, the crew seemed to do a lot of partying that involved drugs, cheap beer, and recreational sex. But Jessie wasn't included, nor did she want to be. Her own salad days were long gone. Cell phones didn't work at sea, and Wi-Fi was expensive and sporadic. For the first time in her life, she was completely on her own in this tiny hermit's cell, afloat on a vast wasteland of salty water.

She opened the drawer of her bedside table and took out some

photos of Kat and her parents. She had selected ones taken during the days when all three had been healthy and happy. The
challenge before her was to replace the images in her brain of
them suffering and dying in hospital beds with these images
of them smiling in the sunlight. But was it possible to banish
your grief without also destroying your memories of past plea-
sures? If you amputated a portion of your heart, wouldn't the
whole organ cease to function?

One photo featured Kat with her arm around Jessie, who was
half a foot shorter than she. But both had silver hair, summer
tans, and high cheekbones. And both were dressed in jeans and
colorful cotton shirts. It was no wonder strangers had often asked
them if they were sisters. At least part of their mutual attraction
must have involved narcissism.

Not for the first time she pondered the fact that both Kat
and her mother had had amber eyes, tinted with the hues of an
autumnal forest. She used to tease them that werewolves had
amber irises, which turned blue when they killed someone. A
recent article in one of her medical journals reported that a high
percentage of heterosexuals picked partners with eye colors identical to those of their opposite-sex parents. Many lesbians, in contrast, picked partners with eyes the same color as their mothers'.
Just in case anyone still believed in free will.

Returning the photos to her drawer, Jessie switched off her
light, rolled over, and wrapped her arms around her pillow, pretending it was Kat. But this comfort was short-lived because it
immediately summoned a flashback to Kat's last days, when she
had been in such pain.

No longer able to swallow, Kat was being fed through a tube that
went directly into her stomach. She was stoic about her own death. Her
lawyer father in North Carolina, an Atticus Finch look-alike, had

worked for Legal Aid in Atlanta as a young man. He had joined the Freedom Riders and had been brained with a lead pipe in Montgomery. His ancestors were Dutch and German farmers who had fought for the Union army during the Civil War. He insisted that he was also part Cherokee. He maintained that many "white" southern families had some African ancestry. But they tried to explain away the darker complexions of various family members by claiming to have had a Cherokee princess for a great-grandmother. He told his children that their ancestors did include Africans, but also a Cherokee woman who had escaped the Trail of Tears by marrying one of the Dutch farmers. As a child, Kat had been entranced by this Cherokee woman and had read everything she could find about her tribe. She had learned that Cherokees taught their children not to cry by holding their nostrils shut, since silence was essential when hiding from enemies. Experimenting, Kat had discovered that it was impossible both to cry and to breathe through your mouth at the same time.

Billions of people had died before her, Kat had pointed out. Billions more would die after her. Everyone died eventually. The only variables were time, place, and cause. One afternoon she asked Jessie to get her feeding tube removed and to give her the maximum doses of morphine so she could starve and dehydrate in repose. Jessie dutifully carried out these wishes.

Kat's last words to her had been "Don't mourn for me too long, Jess. Find someone new and be happy again." Then she pinched her nostrils shut and rolled over, turning her back to Jessie. Friends and family came and went, but she appeared to be in a coma. After a few days she just stopped breathing.

But where is Kat now? Jessie asked herself as she clutched her pillow to her chest. Surely such a forceful personality couldn't just evaporate into thin air? She had asked Kat to send her a sign. No sign had yet arrived. Jessie hadn't been formally religious since she was obliged by her mother to attend the Congregational church in Burlington as a child, but a passage from the Bible kept scrolling through her brain: "For now we see through a glass darkly: but then face to face." Will I ever again see Kat face-to-face? she wondered as the ship rolled slowly back and forth on its giant belly. Not likely. But anyone currently alive who pretended to know the answer to this question was lying.

RUSTY KINCAID DUCKED THROUGH A NARROW DOORWAY off the walking deck. Before him rose eight extra ship propellers, each eight feet high and eight feet wide. They were made of textured stainless steel that glistened in the moonlight. Shaped like sharks' fins with rounded points, they were called "the Commodore's Cuff Links." They could have passed for abstract sculptures. The wall beyond them was low enough to climb over, and far below lay the open sea. At that moment the water was being whipped by the wind into racing white horse tails, illuminated by light falling from the dining room windows. He couldn't say yet when he would jump, but late one night before this cruise ended, so would his life.

He tried to imagine that final plunge. Would his body take over and struggle to surface, or would it agree just to sink down into the inky depths? Would sharks arrive to rip him apart, or would he continue to sink until he rested on the ocean floor with the barnacled hulls of sunken ships and the grinning skulls of drowned sailors?

His mother and sisters had taken up a collection to send him on this cruise. Their hope was that he would meet a nice woman who would help him recover from Irene. He first met Irene when she signed up for golf lessons with him at the Cincinnati country club. What he noticed right away were the crow's-feet around her eyes when she removed her sunglasses and the deep laugh lines etched into either side of her mouth. "A mature face," his mother and sisters had called it. But a sensual face was what he saw. Her golf lessons had lengthened to include drinks in the bar afterward. Then drinks and dinner. Then drinks, dinner, and the bed in his apartment above the pro shop. He had never been so in love. But after five months she went back to her boring hedge-fund husband. Rusty had tried to drown his heartbreak in pot and alcohol. He had been in and out of rehab twice and had taken several brands of antidepressants. He had lost his job.

Once on the ship, Rusty had obediently attended the singles gatherings in the piano lounge before lunchtime. Plenty of eager women had flocked around him. But none was Irene. He had done therapy, so he understood his plight: He was the youngest of six children. His parents and all his siblings had doted on him. He was his mother's favorite. He had been a golf champion at an early age and was said to be good-looking, to boot. Women had thrown themselves at him, but he had rarely responded because most wanted a breadwinner. Whereas what he wanted was a woman who would coddle him as his mother and older sisters had done. Irene, the mother of four, had held out the promise of being that woman. But then she had ditched him, saying that her own needy children were more than enough for her.

The walking deck had become an obsession with Rusty. He spent his days circling the ship like a dog trying to locate a place to lie down, searching for the best spot from which to jump. If he jumped from the balcony of his cabin, he would land in a lifeboat. If he jumped from the bow, where Leonardo DiCaprio and Kate Winslet had spooned on the *Titanic,* the officers on the bridge would spot him and initiate maneuvers to avoid sucking him into the propellers. They would turn the ship around to retrieve him. He needed to find a place where no one would see him, not even the CCTV cameras. He had to make sure he wasn't rescued and resuscitated and returned to the torment that had plagued him every minute of every day since Irene had abandoned him. The low wall by the Commodore's Cuff Links held the promise of being that perfect spot.

Rusty returned to the walking deck. As he passed other chatting passengers, the phrase kept running through his head in time to his footsteps, "I want to be dead. I want to be dead." The truth was, he didn't really want to be dead. He just wanted this relentless pain to stop. But he had tried everything else. Apparently the only way to end the pain was to end his life. Making this decision had already helped him feel better. One day soon this long heartbreak would cease.

But he still felt an obligation to his mother and sisters at least to try to enjoy this cruise they had financed, until he just couldn't bear it anymore, so he entered the ship at the doorway that led to the ballroom, where the Arabian Nights Gala was now in full swing.

ATTIRED IN HER EMBROIDERED GREEN GALABIYA, WITH A long silk scarf thrown around her neck and over one shoulder, Gail stood at the edge of the dance floor in the ship's ballroom while the orchestra onstage played "Fly Me to the Moon." A woman with tousled auburn hair was singing jauntily into the microphone in an impressive alto voice.

Gail scanned the dancers for Harry, a gentleman host she had met at the singles meeting that morning in the piano lounge. Most men there had been "hosts," who received free passage in return for dancing and playing Scrabble with the many single women on board. They wore small rectangular pins that identified them as gigolos of the high seas. Harry was the most presentable of those hosts, in a well-cut Italian suit. His hair was quite thin on top, but balding was said to be a symptom of excess testosterone, and what woman could object to that? Gail was determined to discover whether Harry's services extended beyond Scrabble.

Gail spotted Harry, now disguised as a Bedouin sheikh in a white robe and a red-checked kaffiyeh. He was dancing with a woman from the singles meeting who wore filmy pink harem pants and a face veil. Gail felt a stab of indignation. Had Harry already paired off without even auditioning her? But as far as she was concerned, couples were created to be split up. A triangle was her favorite geometric shape. She adored it when both halves of a previously devoted couple could be beguiled into preferring her to each other.

Meanwhile, Gail spotted another man from the singles meeting who wasn't a host. He was tall and lanky, with curly ginger hair. No corny costume, thank God, just a nice seersucker suit and what appeared to be a Ralph Lauren Black Label tie. He was sitting alone at a small round table, looking as downcast as a rock star whose band has just quit. The challenge of cheering him up appealed to her. He seemed quite young, but she realized she would rather baby-sit him than nurse Charles.

Poor Charles had nothing to recommend him anymore. She had heard the saga of Okinawa so many times that she could have recited it while in a coma. He kept pointing out that he belonged to the Greatest Generation. Finally she asked him why, if he was so great, he couldn't get it up? She had lived for years in a state of arousal that sent her on the prowl whenever she had the chance. It was such a sad contrast to their courtship, when she had been in charge of his young children and he had had to waylay her during naps and after bedtime—once his wife had passed out from too many vodka tonics. He had enjoyed this regimen of deceit and had shown no intention of getting a divorce. So she had finally been forced to leave one of his love notes to her on the kitchen counter.

She sauntered up to the gloomy young man's table. "May I join you?"

He gave her a wan smile and stood up to pull out a chair. Then he sat back down and gazed at her without enthusiasm.

"I'm Gail."

"Rusty." He extended his hand, and they shook.

Gail noted that it was a tanned hand with a firm grip. Flexible fingers were always a plus in a man.

"Would you like a drink?" he asked.

"A scotch would be nice, thanks."

He looked all around, spotted a waiter, and waved him over.

"Didn't I see you at the singles meeting this morning?" asked Gail.

He nodded.

"Where are you from?"

"Cincinnati."

"Are you having fun on our cruise?"

He nodded, though his mournful spaniel eyes contradicted him.

"Do you dance?"

He shook his head.

This was going to require some heavy lifting, reflected Gail. But sometimes the shy ones could be the most passionate. Their feelings were so pent-up that, once released, they could turn into a raging torrent of lust. Rusty might relax once he understood that she didn't want marriage or money from him, just some uncomplicated sex.

"My husband is sick in bed with norovirus," she announced, to put him at ease.

He looked alarmed instead.

"Don't worry, I'm not contagious. I've already had it and have recovered."

The waiter placed their drinks on their little table.

"What do you do in Cincinnati?"

"I used to be a golf pro."

"Really? I love golf. Maybe you could give me some pointers?"

He nodded. "Of course."

The orchestra started playing "Moon River."

"I adore this song," said Gail, sighing. "Are you sure you won't dance with me?"

He hesitated for a long moment. "I guess I could try."

They stood up and walked out on the dance floor. Their bodies fit together well. Gail was imagining what a handsome couple they must appear to Harry, the faithless escort, who was waltzing nearby with a different member of his harem, without even a glance in Gail's direction.

After "Moon River," Rusty and Gail cha-chaed to "La Bamba" and shagged to "Runaround Sue." Sweating and out of breath, they fell into each other's arms for "Smoke Gets in Your Eyes." Gail pressed her breasts against Rusty's chest. He pulled her close with his hand in the small of her back, and she could feel his erection.

Praise the Lord, she thought. From a man who can't get it up to a man who can't keep it down, and all in one night!

"You're too modest, Rusty," she whispered in his ear. "You dance wonderfully."

———

HARRY WATCHED THE GORGEOUS BLOND WOMAN HE'D
spotted that morning at the singles meeting. He had hoped to
ask her to dance tonight, but she appeared fully engaged with
a rangy redheaded golf pro who had also attended the meeting.
The rule was that he couldn't dance twice in a row with the same
woman. He was supposed to entertain all the single women on
board without showing favoritism.

This was an easy assignment for him, since he had been a
priest. He knew how to sublimate lust. He had been doing it
successfully for years when Sister Estelle appeared before his altar
rail in her black-and-white habit. Kneeling, she accepted the
host from him with lowered eyes. Day after day she returned.
One morning she raised smoldering green eyes to meet his. His
fingers trembled as he placed the host on her outstretched tongue.

Eventually both endured the scandal of leaving the Church to
marry each other. He had been terrified, since he knew no other
way to earn a living. But even then, before all the revelations
about predator priests, he had felt contempt for his colleagues
who violated their vows of celibacy yet continued to ride the
Church gravy train—such as the priest in his Maryland hometown who fathered a child with his housekeeper and then turned
the child over to her sister to raise. Or the priest in the neighboring town who employed a "houseboy" who was actually his lover.
He had first encountered this form of hypocrisy in seminary when
some of his fellow students had justified playing musical beds
with one another by defining celibacy to mean the avoidance of
a long-term relationship that might detract from one's commit-
ment to God and to one's parishioners. Under this definition a
succession of one-night stands was okay.

But he and Estelle had bitten the bullet and forfeited their status, their vocations, and their livelihoods for each other, unwilling to conceal or deny their love. He opened an insurance agency, and they took up ballroom dancing with an avidity available only to those who have been prohibited from dancing for much of their lives. They won a number of competitions all over the United States. But after twenty idyllic years, Estelle developed breast cancer and died. Since he had retired from his insurance agency to take care of her, he was dreadfully lonely afterward. So he signed up as a gentleman host on the *Amphitrite* for companionship. With his dance experience, he met their most important requirement. Now he cruised much of the year, sharing a cabin with another host and spending his days and evenings entertaining single women with bridge, Trivial Pursuit, and spirited mealtime banter.

Many made passes at him, but he abided by his agreement with the cruise line not to get involved with any one particular woman on board. Should he do so, he would be asked to leave the ship, and this comfortable, convivial life he had created for himself would end. But sometimes when he got back home between cruises, women from the ship stopped by his Maryland condo to quench desires that had been provoked by all that shipboard restraint.

Chapter 3

Reverse Cowgirl

"THIS IS YOUR CAPTAIN SPEAKING. IT'S A LOVELY AFTER-noon here on the Arabian Sea. The waters are calm, with just the slightest swell, and a gentle breeze from the northwest is keeping the temperature balmy on deck. I think you would be hard-pressed not to agree with me that it's a glorious season to be seaborne—and a marvelous day simply to be alive!"

As she ate spinach ravioli in the officers' dining room, Jessie smiled at Captain Kilgore's British accent, combined with his un-British rhapsodies about the weather. His daily noontime commentaries usually sounded like bad bucolic poetry. At age forty-six, he had recently married for the first time—a younger French woman who sold Hermès scarves in a boutique on board. She was always decked out in her wares, and she ran workshops to teach women passengers four dozen ways to tie their scarves, like sailors learning their knots. The captain appeared here and there around the ship all day long, sporting a goofy grin. He was so besotted with his new wife that it was a wonder he could steer the ship in a straight line.

Loud laughter erupted from a table in the corner, at which

huddled four bridge officers in white uniforms and a young East Indian woman who worked behind the purser's desk. Clearly the men were vying for her favors. The male to female ratio among the staff, officers, and crew was about five to one, so the women on board were wielding unaccustomed power. Since each officer had his own cabin, they were prime targets. Even if they had wives back home, many of the men had no scruples about also having what were called "ship mistresses." The women themselves enjoyed the spacious cabins and the gifts from the duty-free boutiques—and hopefully the illicit lovemaking, as well.

The ship itself was organized like the British Empire. On the top decks were the suites that housed aristocrats, film stars, politicians, and wealthy businessmen. On the decks below were the commoners who had saved for years to afford their passage. And below sea level, crammed four into each windowless cabin, were the people who did all the work, most from the Philippines, though the cruise literature stated that the crew represented some sixty-five countries.

Returning to her cabin, Jessie watched out her window as the skyline of Dubai gradually appeared on the horizon. She was listening to Otis Redding sing "I've Been Loving You Too Long (To Stop Now)" through earbuds attached to her iPhone. Kat had also loved this song. Jessie had listened to it several times a day ever since her death. It certainly summed up Jessie's current predicament.

The clinic was currently closed because half the passengers were disembarking in Dubai to fly home, and the other half were going on shore excursions. Captain Kilgore had already emphasized over the loudspeaker that many new passengers from northern climes would no doubt be bringing viruses on board—instead of acknowledging that his ship had already become a hothouse for norovirus. The *Amphitrite* should probably have been flying a black flag, like the plague ships in the fourteenth century.

Dubai was wedged between the desert and the ocean. A mist of salt spray and fine sand shrouded it in a tremulous haze. As the ship slowly approached the port, dozens of giant skyscrapers seemed to rise right up out of the sea like a shimmering mirage. The tallest building in the world pierced this haze like a spear. Alongside it sat lower buildings, one built to resemble the wind-swollen sail of a dhow.

Using its side thrusters, the ship sidled up to the quay. Seamen appeared fore and aft to attach long rope cables the thickness of Jessie's forearm to the cleats. Then they placed round collars of tin around the ropes to prevent rats from scurrying up them into the holds. If someone had only thought to put collars around mooring ropes in the fourteenth century, mused Jessie, rats with fleas that carried the plague couldn't have spread it. There would have been no Black Death. For want of a few thousand tin disks, 25 million people had died.

Jessie retrieved from her desk the handout from the purser about which body parts needed to be concealed in Dubai—as though the sight of her swollen ankles in her white nurse's oxfords might drive the local men into a frenzy of lust. It seemed that shoulders and knees were forbidden in Dubai, so no shorts or tank tops. Apparently the head and hair could remain uncovered. Also, the sheet warned, no public displays of affection, and especially not homosexual ones, which could result in imprisonment or deportation. Living for so many years in Vermont, where homosexuals were regarded as normal everyday taxpaying citizens, had shielded Jessie from the reality almost everywhere else. But this cruise was serving to remind her that she and her friends might yet be herded into boxcars or machine-gunned into mass graves.

This condemnation of homosexuality in Dubai seemed especially hypocritical coming from people who had owned slaves until 1963. A blogger on the Internet that morning had claimed that the elite here paid their former slaves to attend their parties because it was a status symbol to display how many you had once owned. The blogger also claimed that on the desert outskirts of this city stood concrete barracks with no air-conditioning that housed 300,000 men from India and Bangladesh, lured here with the promise of high wages for construction jobs. When these wages didn't materialize, they were unable to return home because their passports had been confiscated by their employers. Apparently most of the amazing structures composing the Dubai skyline had been built by such captive labor.

But Jessie reminded herself that if she insisted on itemizing the crimes of every port at which the ship docked, she would just make herself miserable. Kat had trained her to notice the broader political implications of her experiences. But their children, Anthony and Cady, Martin and Malcolm, hypnotized by tiny electronic screens that merely reflected them back to themselves smaller than life, had no such difficulties. And if she wanted to rejoin the carefree, she would probably do better to concentrate on the theme of life as a Mardi Gras in this Las Vegas of the Persian Gulf.

Jessie pulled on cargo pants and a long-sleeved khaki shirt with many tabs and flaps and zippers, plus a wide-brimmed hat with a chin strap. Her face would be her only flesh on display for the ravaging males of Dubai. Looking into her mirror, she was disappointed to discover that she resembled Harrison Ford in *Raiders of the Lost Ark* more than Katharine Hepburn in *The*

African Queen. She noted with dismay a new splotch of sun damage that had just appeared on her right cheek, joining several others. The only good thing about her increasing number of facial wrinkles was that they concealed some of the dark spots. Apparently all those childhood summers on the glaring waters of Lake Champlain were now staking their claim.

She boarded a shuttle bus in the bustling port, which was stacked high with multicolored metal shipping containers, like a child's Lego project. In the city, she toured a museum in an old adobe fort with exhibits that concerned the founding of the town by fishermen and smugglers. Antique photos showed robed and veiled women carrying huge pottery water jars on their heads in the spot where the tallest building in the world now loomed. You had to admire whatever forces had conspired to allow the women of Dubai to abandon their giant water jugs for indoor plumbing, and to trade their burkas for Versace and Armani.

Jessie rode a converted fishing boat across a creek to the gold souk, where she wandered along the main corridor, surrounded by tourists inflamed with lust for the gold gewgaws that filled the display windows and flowed out the shop doors as though from Ali Baba's caves. She spotted Ben Armstrong, wearing khakis and a black polo shirt. He had a cleft in his chin, as well as dimples in his cheeks when he smiled. Before their affair, she had fantasized about caressing those facial craters with her tongue. The reality had been disappointing. His thick stubble had chafed her tongue, lips, and cheeks like coarse sandpaper. That was the trouble with trying to enact your fantasies. Either they turned out to be boring, or the gymnastics required to achieve them proved impossible to perform without dislocating a limb. She recalled her first and last threesome, in Vermont during commune days, which had concluded with sheepish apologies all around. She had long since discovered that it was more arousing to leave the imaginary within your imagination.

Ben's problem was that he was too good-looking. Women had always pursued him, so he had never learned how to be agreeable. He now had four disgruntled ex-wives and six estranged children to support, without a clue as to why the wives had all left him. He had taken the *Amphitrite* gig because it paid hardship wages and there was almost nothing to squander them on—if you stayed away from the ship's casino and from Dubai's gold souk. You also had no expenses for rent, food, clothing, utilities, health care, or liability insurance. In addition, staff were forbidden to fraternize with "guests," as the cruise line insisted their employees refer to passengers. So even if Ben yearned for wife number five, he wasn't likely to corral her without getting thrown off the ship.

"So how's it going, Jessie?" Ben sauntered toward her. He held up both hands, palms out, to indicate that he knew a welcoming hug between them might get them both deported. "Did you ever imagine there was this much gold in the entire solar system?"

"It's pretty amazing, all right."

"Are you going to buy something?"

"God no!"

Ben laughed. "You're probably the only woman I know who would say that."

"I'm trying to get rid of stuff, not acquire more."

"I could buy you a memento of our cruise—a bauble for your charm bracelet?"

"Save it for your alimony payments."

"That's what I've always loved about you, Jessie. No muss, no fuss, no bother. How come we never got married?"

"It might have something to do with the fact that I'm a lesbian."

"You're no lesbian—if my memory serves me correctly. You must be at least bisexual?"

Jessie smiled. "I'm not anything anymore—just a grieving widow. The children nowadays have invented all these labels— tranny, cis, shemale, boi, bisexual, pansexual, polyamorous, queer, top, bottom, nonbinary. As far as I'm concerned, they should do and be whatever they please. But they need to get over themselves and realize that Syrian refugees are drowning in the Mediterranean."

"Yikes!" said Ben. "Somebody's grumpy today."

"Well, it's just that all that gender-identity stuff isn't really very important because everyone's body—whatever its gender or nongender—still collapses and decays in the end."

"Hmmm. So you're sad, and I'm sad, too. How about a little mutual comfort in the night?"

"Not gonna happen," Jessie assured him. The thing about having grown up in Vermont in the seventies, in that golden age after the invention of the Pill and before the arrival of HIV, was that you had already tried everything, so you lacked the curiosity that might propel you into disastrous new explorations. "And you know perfectly well that if you had me again, Ben, you'd soon grow tired of me, just as you have of all the others. That would make me furious. I might take a scalpel to you, and then have to spend my final years in prison, being raped by scary women. So it's better if we just stay friends."

Ben laughed. "Yow! I see your point!"

"But you're very sweet to pretend that you want me. Especially since I feel about as desirable right now as a corpse on an autopsy slab."

Ben grimaced.

"I suggest you get yourself a massage at the spa instead," said Jessie. "There are some lovely women there with very strong hands."

"I already tried that. My masseuse wanted to marry a rich doctor and move to the States. By the time she got through with me, I almost agreed. But I need a fifth wife almost as much as I need a pet skunk."

BEN WATCHED JESSIE STRIDE DOWN THE CORRIDOR OF THE souk toward the ship, looking like a petite Dr. Livingston in her safari gear. She was small but very wiry, as he recalled from their trysts at Roosevelt Hospital. Her biceps had been at least as firm as his, and she had been able to pin him with ease. Not that he had ever opposed her being on top.

She had captured his attention the first time he ever saw her—in pale blue scrubs with coal black hair in a pixie cut, her eyes as blue as the sea on a sunny autumn morning. Now her hair had gone silver, and her face bore the wrinkles and discolorations appropriate to her age. But her eyes were just as vivid as before—and as remote. Even when she had been his lover, he had never felt as though he had any hold over her. She possessed a detachment that he had found alluring at first, evoking his love of a challenge, but in the end it had proved impossible to breach.

Ben had met her parents when they came to visit her at Roosevelt. Her mother, as diminutive as Jessie, was movie-star beautiful. Her amber eyes were as cruel as those of Queen Grimhilde in *Snow White.* Her father was a urologist, world-famous for his nerve-sparing innovations in surgery for prostate cancer. He was also a war hero who walked with a cane because of his injuries.

As they toured the corridors of the hospital, several of the older doctors and nurses recognized him and behaved as though they were experiencing an Elvis sighting.

Dr. and Mrs. Drake were staying at the Erie Hotel on West Fifty-sixth Street, where they had rendezvoused after his ship home from the war in Europe had docked in New York City. At that time he had qualified for a discount because he had worked as a surgeon for the Erie Railroad right after medical school. By the time they visited Jessie, though, the Erie had been converted into a welfare hotel. But Dr. and Mrs. Drake had been enchanted by the cheap room rate. Dr. Drake had invited Ben and Jessie to lunch, and had then treated them to a hot dog from a street cart. Mrs. Drake said almost nothing the entire time, eyeing Ben with cool dislike, having evidently figured out that he and her daughter had been sharing bodily fluids outside of wedlock.

Ben was alarmed to feel a twinge of attraction to Jessie again. He had offered her the clinic job because he had thought she was safe. They had had their moment in the sun and had quickly fallen back to Earth all those years ago. But at this point he would probably be turned on by anyone with two X chromosomes.

However, he wasn't usually interested in women his own age. That had always been his curse. He had pursued each of his wives because she was a lubricious young vixen. But once married, each had insisted on having a child. When a wife became a mommy, her sex appeal flew out the window for him. A woman could hide her lack of desire for a man, and even feign enthusiasm. But a man's lack of passion was right there on display. He pursued affairs during his marriages because the danger and novelty restored the erections he lost once he became Daddy. Sometimes the excitement of a new affair could even flog a response out of him when he was back in bed with Mommy.

But the mommies always began demanding that he wear their new baby in a sling across his chest while they strolled in Central Park. The saddest sight of all for him was that of a young man trying to jog while pushing a baby stroller. His mother had always taken care of her household and her children, welcoming Ben's father home at night to a hot meal and a snooze on the couch in front of the TV. But Ben's wives had each expected him—however exhausted from pumping stomachs all day long—to give their children baths and read them inane bedtime stories involving talking animals. Young women now were spoiled princesses, demanding not only their own credit cards but also assistance with rearing the children and doing the housework. How had so many men allowed this to occur?

He asked himself why things hadn't worked out with Jessie back in the Roosevelt days. If he couldn't have a wife who would take care of him, at least he could have picked one who could take care of herself. He remembered their groping around inside each other's scrubs in supply closets all over the hospital—and visits to her tiny apartment across the street in a redbrick Italianate building with arched windows, a bracketed cornice, and a rooftop campanile. Apparently her parents had lived in this same building when her father was at Roosevelt after the war. She claimed to have been conceived on the fourth floor—though Ben found it hard to imagine that her chilly mother would ever have parted her knees for any man. Jessie used to say that she was like a monarch butterfly, returning to the site of her hatching. Both he and she had usually been so exhausted by their inhuman schedules at the hospital that they merely lay down in each other's arms and slept chastely.

The truth was, Ben had never really wanted to be a doctor. As a child, he had received at Christmas and birthdays tiny scrubs and miniature medical instruments, which he had halfheartedly employed on his sisters' dolls, while his sisters shrieked in protest. At dinner every night his father had described in sickening detail the operations he had performed that day. But at Amherst, Ben had been more interested in archaeology—other times and distant places, not the urgent here and now of medicine—although he did take the premed prerequisites. In a feeble gesture toward self-determination, he had fled to Steamboat, Colorado, after graduation, teaching skiing by day and waiting tables at night. But gradually he had acceded to his father's wishes, taking the MCATs, applying to med schools, and somehow managing to get accepted at Cornell.

Medicine had proved an okay way to earn a living. But he would love to retire now and volunteer on some archaeological digs before he became too infirm to wield a shovel. Though that wouldn't be possible anytime soon with four alimony payments and six children to put through college. What in the world had he been thinking? He hadn't been thinking. He just hadn't known how to keep his pecker in his pocket.

It was probably because Jessie and he had had no time for romance that theirs hadn't flourished. When the gossip reached him that she was with a woman, he had refused to believe it. And now he felt certain he could persuade her to change her mind. She was perfect for him: She had her own income, and she was well past menopause. And women rarely turned him down if he put his mind to it.

JESSIE DODGED THE LINES OF EMBARKING PASSENGERS AND their luggage as she reboarded the *Amphitrite*. She walked fast down the central corridor on the first deck, which the crew called "I-95," thinking about Ben and his clumsy come-on. Even if good sense told her he was nothing but a sexual opportunist, it still cheered her up to think that he might find her attractive, since she currently felt half-dead from having so recently accompanied three loved ones to the brink of extinction. Sexual predation and assault were one thing, but a little pointless flirtation was the Tabasco sauce on the gumbo of life. Criminalizing it was like exterminating the rats in your cellar with a Molotov cocktail.

She had several male friends, and she hoped she could convert Ben into one of those. First, though, all the men had had to recover from their incredulity that some women might actually prefer to make love to other women, with no penis in sight. But for many women there was an undeniable relief in being able to focus on mutual pleasure, rather than on the capricious hydraulics of a penis.

Her only once-male friend who understood this without a struggle was a trans surgical nurse in Burlington named Elle. She said when potential boyfriends learned that she had happily forfeited her penis, most searched for an exit door right away. She also said that when her body had appeared to be male, people had praised her every utterance. But once she transitioned, she was constantly challenged and criticized. She had been forced too late to face the fact that being a woman wasn't all it had been cracked up to be.

Jessie was just grateful that transitioning hadn't been an option when she was young. She had been a hard-core tomboy and might have been tempted by that option. But she would have hated to miss out on being a lesbian.

Reaching the clinic, Jessie discovered a young man with

ginger curls sprawled on the linoleum outside the doorway. He looked like one of the Rolling Stones before alcohol and drugs had transformed them into elderly haints.

He peered up at her through bloodshot eyes and croaked, "Is the clinic open?"

"I'm just now opening it. But what's happened to you?"

"I think I've broken something." His voice was almost a whisper.

Jessie unlocked the door and helped him to his feet. Inside, she handed him a patient questionnaire and a pen. He sat down gingerly in a chair in the waiting area and began to fill it out. After he returned it to her, she escorted him into an examining room. They sat down. "So what do you think you've broken, Mr. Kincaid?"

He blushed deep red. "Uh. Is it possible to break your . . . uh . . . penis?"

"Well, there's no bone there. But you can rupture one of the tubes that cause erections. Did you hear a popping sound?"

He nodded miserably.

"Did you lose your erection?"

He nodded.

"Are you bruised and swollen down there?"

He nodded.

"I'd better take a look." She handed him a robe. "Remove your trousers and underwear and drape yourself with this. I'll be back shortly."

Amy had arrived at the reception desk, and the waiting area was filling up with patients. Jessie motioned for Amy to accompany her to the examining room. Male patients always got nervous when she examined their genitalia. She tried her best to help them understand that their penises were of no more interest to her than were hernias. In fact, the great unspoken secret was that most women loved their men in spite of their wheedling appendages. The idea that a woman could be seduced by texting her a photo of your erect penis made most women howl with nervous laughter. Given that a quarter of all women had been raped, it was as tone-deaf as texting a photo of a noose to an African-American. It was almost as clueless as the porn industry's depictions of what two women do in bed together.

Jessie removed the robe from the young man's lap and discovered a genital area gone entirely black-and-blue, and a swollen penis the shape of a small papaya. "Oh my! That must really hurt. We need to get you into surgery in Dubai as soon as possible."

"Surgery?" he gasped. "Could I lose my penis?"

"No. Don't worry. A urologist needs to do an MRI or an ultrasound to see if you've damaged your urethra. And he'll have to take a few stitches to patch up your torn tube. But you'll soon be fine. However, I'm afraid the ship can't wait for you. I hope you took out trip insurance? Go to your cabin and pack your things. Get your passport from the purser and ask Guest Services to arrange a flight home for you. Bring your valuables and medications and meet me on the quay. Your cabin steward will carry your luggage out."

Jessie paged Ben. He was still in the gold souk, buying mementos for his daughters. She explained what had happened. He replied that he would contact a urologist in Dubai and page her back with instructions.

AS RUSTY THREW HIS BELONGINGS INTO HIS SUITCASE, HE was upset over his injury. But he was especially upset that he would have to abandon Gail Savage without an explanation. They had really hit it off, and he had glimpsed the promise of at last recovering from Irene. Back at his cabin after the Arabian Nights Gala, Gail had claimed she wanted his help with her golf swing. He had stood behind her and guided the lift of her arms, the angle of her wrists, the twist of her hips as she employed an imaginary club. One thing had led to another, and soon she was teaching him positions from the *Kama Sutra*. He had to admit that they were more engaging than variations on golf strokes. But then Gail had insisted on trying what she called "the Reverse Cowgirl," and all hell had broken loose. Still, he realized that he owed Gail his life. If he hadn't met her, he would probably have ducked into that nook where the Commodore's Cuff Links were stored and jumped overboard.

Gail had said she was on a world cruise. Maybe he could re-board the ship at an upcoming port. For the first time since Irene had dumped him, he found himself grinning. His aching groin was proof that he was back in the saddle again!

PEDRO ENTERED MR. KINCAID'S ROOM TO RETRIEVE HIS luggage. As he picked up the suitcase and carry-on, he tried to figure out what was wrong with this man who seemed so much like a little boy. Here he was on a trip that cost more than Pedro earned in two years, but he just sat around looking miserable. He and Mr. Kincaid were probably the same age, but Pedro already had a wife and two small children back in the Philippines. He saw them for only two months a year, in between cruises. Sometimes, if a passenger gave him a phone card as a tip, he would call home from a port. Otherwise, he stayed on this ship for ten months at a time, working twelve hours a day, seven days a week.

Any time off was spent in the crew bar or in the small cabin he shared with three other Filipino stewards.

It was a difficult life, but he was grateful to have work that allowed him to support his family. Before the Spaniards arrived, his ancestors had sailed all around Southeast Asia on merchant vessels. During the Spanish occupation, they had been forced to sail for Spain. In the nineteenth century, they had worked on American whaling vessels. His father had also worked on cruise ships. Pedro was proud to uphold this family tradition, however lonely and demanding.

Pedro was like a second father to many of the younger Filipino workers. He tried to explain to them the need to act respectful toward passengers, even when you despised them. That was how you earned tips and phone cards. But the younger men had a hard time faking it. Behind the guests' backs they called them "Coneheads," after a family of aliens on American TV who consumed vast quantities of food, including cleaning fluid and insulation.

But Pedro had even changed his name to maximize his tips. The guests couldn't pronounce or remember his real name, Gualterio. It meant "strong warrior" in his own language, and his mother had picked it on purpose to inspire him to be brave and bold. But he told the guests just to call him Pedro. A few insisted on learning how to pronounce Gualterio. He always put extra foil-wrapped chocolates on their pillows when he turned down their covers at night. But most guests were relieved just to call him Pedro and slip him more free phone cards.

Pedro watched over his younger countrymen during all their foolishness. Because there weren't many women on board, the stewards, cleaners, and waiters, those who worked in maintenance and in the engine room and the kitchens, didn't often get them. The women chose the officers, who could offer them single rooms at night and buy them perfume at the boutiques. Some crew resorted to chi-chi men, who would let other men screw them. But most just drank too many cheap Coronas in the crew bar. Some brought cocaine and pot on board in the soles of their shoes. What they couldn't sell to passengers, they used themselves. They spent their free time in a stupor, reminiscing about the whores in Rio who, they claimed, loved Filipino men because the Filipinos didn't treat them like whores.

He would laugh and say, "Don't fool yourselves, boys. They want your money, just like whores anywhere else."

Chapter 4

Too Close to the Ground

THROUGH THE CLINIC PORTHOLE JESSIE COULD SEE THE Muscat harbor, surrounded by jagged gunmetal gray mountains. On a cliff stood the tumbled stone ruins of a Portuguese fort from colonial days, when Muscat had become wealthy from the transport to the Middle East of slaves captured in East Africa. The buildings of the city were low and bright white, with crenellated walls and wooden balconies. Palm trees swayed in a salty breeze.

Across the street at the entrance to the souk stood men dressed in collarless white gowns and round embroidered caps. There were almost no women in sight. Probably they had all stayed home to bleach, starch, and iron those blindingly white gowns. The few women Jessie did spot wore long black abayas, with veils across their faces. White reflected heat and black trapped it, so it made sense to Jessie that women in these Islamic desert countries were required to wear black body bags while their menfolk wore airy white gowns.

Still, that morning Jessie had watched on the sputtering Internet some Victoria's Secret models doing a fashion show in China. They wore patterned stockings on their flamingo legs,

with skimpy lace thongs and bras and garter belts, all roped
together by spiderwebs of black leather straps, like bondage gear.
Comparing them to these Arab women in their black pup tents,
she was hard-pressed to say which group was in reality less free.

Farther down the quay she could see the turquoise and golden
mushroom columns of the ceremonial palace of the Omani sultan.
The gay grapevine back home had long maintained that he kept
an all-male harem and a platoon of handsome young bodyguards.
In addition, he had had an opera house constructed in Muscat,
which the grapevine insisted was proof positive of his orientation.
The grapevine also claimed that homosexuals from throughout
the Arab world were vying to immigrate to Oman and volunteer
for the harem. If you weren't a member of the harem or one of
the bodyguards, you could be imprisoned in Oman for being gay.
But at least you couldn't be executed, as in other sharia-ruled
countries.

Passengers from the *Amphitrite,* dressed in pastel cruise gear,
were milling around the entrance to the souk, like sheep about
to be fleeced. For a moment Jessie thought she spotted the blond
ponytail of Gail Savage. Then she remembered that she had quar-
antined Gail in her cabin with her ill husband. But she realized
that she had forgotten to alert the purser. She picked up the
house phone, dialed the purser, and asked him to deactivate the
keys to room 10024. If the Savages took a notion to disobey her,
they wouldn't be able to get back into their room. She would be
notified and could have them put off the ship.

A man standing behind the counter cleared his throat. As
Jessie looked up, he asked, "Are you open yet?"

"Yes, we are. How can I help you?" The middle-aged man
had a dark five o'clock shadow and a snake tattoo winding up his
muscled right forearm.

"I've sprained my ankle. Maybe broken it." His accent was some variety of British. English, Irish, Scottish, Australian, Canadian, South African—that was about as specific as Jessie could get.

She handed him a clipboard. As he filled out the questionnaire, she went into the exam room and set up the digital X-ray machine. Back at the counter, she looked over his information, ascertaining that Rodney Mullins was from Leeds. A Yorkshire accent. She gestured for him to follow her. He sat on the examining table and pulled up his chino pant leg. As she removed his deck shoe, she could see that he was grimacing. The ankle was swollen and purple. She poked it with her fingertips and carefully moved the foot here and there to check its range of motion. He had walked to the clinic, so it was doubtful the ankle was broken. Nevertheless, she decided to x-ray it, unable to rely on her own intuition, as her grandfather would have done.

"How did this happen?" she asked as she waited for the images to appear on her monitor.

He was carefully replacing his shoe. "I fell down some steps on the observation deck as we were approaching Muscat."

"It must have been crowded up there."

"I was trying to get some photos. Everyone else was, too, so there was some serious jostling."

"Well, the good news is that your ankle isn't broken. I'll wrap it. You should go back to your cabin and elevate your leg with pillows. Every hour or so, ice the ankle for ten minutes. I'll give you some crutches and some acetaminophen for the pain."

AS RODNEY SWUNG OUT OF THE CLINIC ON HIS NEW crutches, he wondered why he hadn't told the nice doctor with the lavender stethoscope around her neck that he had been pushed down those steps. An attractive American woman with a blond ponytail and turquoise eyes had accused him of stealing her place at the railing. This wasn't true, because he had been positioned there for a good half hour before she arrived. He guessed he hadn't mentioned it because he didn't want to seem like a wimp, elbowed aside by a woman.

Rodney had acquired his snake tattoo during a drunken night in Singapore while on R&R from Vietnam. Afterward, his fellow soldiers started calling him "Serp," for serpent. Upon leaving the British army, he had worked as a jewel thief. His boss, who used his own resemblance to David Niven to gain entrance to fancy restaurants, would zero in on people who wore expensive jewelry and would give Serp their details. Serp's job had been to break into their houses, open their safes, and relieve them of the jewels.

Luckily, he hadn't been caught by the time he met Melva. She convinced him to start a business installing and maintaining security systems, an easy transition, since he was already an expert on them. By the time he handed the business over to his son, he was widely known as the premier security provider in Yorkshire.

Now he and Melva traveled the world on the *Amphitrite.* The cruise they were currently taking cost more than their first house. He spent the days in port tanning on a lounge chair at the ship's swimming pool, while Melva went on bus tours. Melva came home at teatime most days, annoyed that the Germans on the tours didn't know how to queue properly. But what Serp loved best were the days at sea, when the gentle rolling of the boat and the Tim McGraw songs on his iPhone lulled him to sleep there in the sun by the sloshing pool. He also loved the daily line-dancing classes in the ballroom, to which he wore his cowboy boots and hat. Hooking his thumbs through his belt loops, he sashayed up and down the gleaming floor in unison with several dozen others, mostly women. The worst thing about his injury was that he wouldn't be able to wear his boots for a while.

Back in his room, he took some pain pills and rang for Pedro to bring an ice pack.

"Oh no, what have you done to your foot, Mr. Serp?" Pedro arranged a frozen gel pack wrapped in a towel around Serp's bandaged ankle.

"Fell down some steps. Clumsy me, eh?"

"So sorry, Mr. Serp."

"Just Serp is fine, Pedro."

"So sorry, Serp. What else can I get you?"

"Nothing else, thanks. I just need to rest."

As Pedro exited, Serp thought about how much he loved being waited on. He had always waited on others—in his business, but also at home, since Melva worked long hours as a secretary at a propane-delivery firm. His parents had also worked day and night in their off-license shop while he was growing up. Yet here was their son, being waited on like a king. That had been the best thing about the British Empire: the inexpensive servants. Here on the *Amphitrite* you could pretend that the empire still existed (though this fantasy now cost you dearly).

Once the ice pack had been on his ankle for ten minutes, he was freezing and decided to lie in the sun at the pool and get future ice packs from the deck boys. He changed into his black Speedo by hopping around the room on his good foot. Pulling on his white terry-cloth robe, he swung out the door on his crutches.

IN THE LAUNDRY ROOM ON THE TENTH FLOOR, GAIL SAVAGE spread out on the ironing board one of Charles's dampened shirts. When they had courted, he had been a dashing older man. Twenty years later, he was just an older man. She despised his stoop when he walked, the slow and deliberate way he flossed his yellowed teeth, the milky film that had clouded his once-burning brown eyes. Why wouldn't he pay to have his damn shirts washed at the laundry? He whined that people other than she used too much starch or folded them incorrectly. He made it clear that since he was paying for this voyage, just as he had paid for everything else in their life together, she could damn well wash and iron his shirts. She slammed the iron down on his navy blue Lacoste shirt and shoved it back and forth, deliberately ironing in some wrinkles. Maybe if she did a terrible job, he would insist on sending them out.

She and Charles were circling the globe in 128 days. This was supposed to be the trip of a lifetime—a second honeymoon was how Charles had billed it. But the other passengers were disgusting. A young South African couple had shown up in their bathrobes for breakfast that morning in the Poseidon Grill, the premier restaurant on the ship. Charles had paid through the nose for the two of them to eat there, away from the riffraff who gobbled like starving hogs at the buffets downstairs. And last night two gay men from a lower deck had been caught naked doing God knows what in the hot tub reserved for Poseidon passengers. Gail had called the purser, complained about AIDS and STDs, and insisted that the tub be drained and disinfected.

A woman in a hot-pink tank top, too-tight short shorts, and flip-flops appeared in the doorway of the laundry room. She eyed the mound of clothes on the counter.

"Someone took my clothes out of the dryer," she announced. She walked over and felt a few items between her fingertips. "Some aren't even dry yet."

"Your cycle had finished," said Gail.

"Did you take them out?"

"Yes."

"You had no right to touch my property."

"You aren't the only one on this ship who wants to wash clothes." Gail looked up from Charles's shirt at the woman, whose face had flamed an unattractive hot-flash red.

"See how much you like it when I handle your clothes." The woman shoved Gail's pile of folded laundry onto the tile floor.

"What? You fucking bitch!" Gail reached out and pressed her hot iron against the woman's forearm.

"Jesus frigging Christ, you bloody moron!" The woman inspected the scalded red triangle forming on her arm. She advanced with her pink fingernails flexed. Gail thrust the iron at her again, like a gladiator's shield.

The woman whirled around, grabbed her clothes, and marched out, saying, "Don't think this is over yet, lady! You'll be hearing from me!"

"I can't wait!" called Gail.

Gail picked her laundry up off the floor and refolded it. Goddamn Aussie, she thought. Nothing but a bunch of convicts.

From a rack hung a midnight blue silk gown with a plunging back. It looked to be about Gail's size. Someone must have pressed it and left it to pick up later, maybe that repulsive Aussie. Gail unhooked it. Raising it high, along with the hangers that held Charles's shirts, she gathered her laundry in her free arm and headed back to her room. Juggling the clothing, she pounded on the door. That annoying dyke doctor, who swaggered around the ship like a lady wrestler, had disabled their room keys to force them to remain in their cabin. But she was damned if she was going to be cooped up in there for days on end with nothing but Charles and his vomit.

Charles opened the door, wearing his blue naval veteran cap. He relieved her of the laundry. "New dress?" He nodded at the blue silk gown.

"Yes, I bought it in the Muscat souk."

"Pretty."

Laying the clothes on the bed for her to deal with, Charles returned to a lounge chair on the glass-fronted balcony. If he had his way, Gail reflected, he would sit there for the entire voyage while she carried him trays of food and stacks of clean clothing. She was nothing to him anymore but a very expensive maid. No one would ever believe that they had once tried every position in the *Kama Sutra.* Now he wouldn't even do the missionary position. She kept urging him to use the Viagra he'd somehow acquired, but he insisted it might give him a heart attack. Time was when a heart attack would have seemed worth it to him in order to enter her properly.

She arranged his clean clothes in his drawers. Then she opened the balcony door and told him she was going to the hairdresser and would bring him his lunch on her way back. He grunted, not even looking up from his book, a history of World War II in the Pacific. She reached across his shoulder, grabbed the book from his hands, and tossed it over the balcony railing. Its pages fluttered like a seagull's wings as it hurtled toward the water. Charles looked up at her, saying nothing. She whirled around and stalked out of the room.

DRAGO WAS A TWENTYSOMETHING FROM CROATIA. HIS DARK hair was shaved all over his head except for the top, where it stuck up in orange spikes. On his feet were black patent-leather ballet slippers. Gail watched him in the mirror as he clipped her hair.

He was telling her about growing up gay, being raped by the more manly boys in his village. He had finally escaped to a career as a coiffeur on cruise ships. He now went back to his village only once a year, to see his elderly parents. His rapists had married, and now looked the other way when he passed them in the street.

Gail had no interest in hearing about any gay activities that didn't involve hairstyling or the decoration of houses. Others in the salon had names like Olga and Bogdan and Wadim. To change the subject to something less repulsive, Gail asked Drago if he and his coworkers roamed the ship at night, looking for people whose blood they could suck.

He smiled, but then he began regaling her with stories of his lurid escapades when the ship docked. He claimed the young men in Sydney were the hottest in the whole world. Sometimes, he continued, passengers went down to the disco in the crew bar. The crew lacked the authority to tell them to leave. Nor did they want to, because sometimes a passenger would insist on visiting one of the secret spots known only to the crew, giving his tour guide a large tip. Crew members were forbidden to fraternize with passengers. If caught, both would be thrown off at the next port. But it was in everyone's best interests not to report one another.

"Like where?" asked Gail.

"Where what?"

"Where are the secret spots?"

"If I told you, I'd have to kill you." Drago giggled.

"But I won't tell anyone."

"No, you won't, because I won't tell you, either!"

"What if I go down to your disco sometime?" mused Gail.

Drago laughed. "Well, I can't stop you, Mrs. Savage. But I should warn you: Lots of the men at those discos are gay."

"But not all?"

"A few swing both ways. And some straights come just for the dancing."

"Well, I might turn up there one of these nights."

"You could get thrown off the ship."

"If I got caught. But danger is part of the thrill, no?"

Drago grinned. "For men, yes. But I thought you ladies liked everything safe and sanitized."

"What makes you think I'm a lady?"

GAIL STOPPED AT THE BUFFET AND FIXED A PLATE FOR Charles, a piece of white fish and lots of salad. Between his high cholesterol and high triglycerides, that was all he could eat.

Back in the cabin, she served Charles his tray on his lounge chair and informed him that she was going to the pool. She suspected he loved this cruise because he had her trapped. She couldn't leave him—unless she wanted to jump overboard, an idea that sometimes tempted her whenever she had to hear yet again about the hardships of life on battleships in the Pacific two thousand years ago.

Gail put on her bikini. She looked at herself in the mirror. Not so bad. Rusty Kincaid certainly hadn't thought so. In the end, though, he had lost his mojo during the Reverse Cowgirl and had whimpered like a big baby that he couldn't continue. She had thrown on her galabiya and marched out his door—and hadn't seen or heard from him since. "Easy come, easy go" was how she categorized such overeager young puppies.

Up on the pool deck, Gail discovered that all the chairs she liked, the ones with soft cushions, had been taken. Either people were sitting in them or they had left towels and books on them. The rule was that if people tried to reserve chairs, you were entitled to hand their stuff to the deck boy and take the chair for yourself.

She studied the chairs, trying to decide whether she wanted to be in the sun or the shade. Finally selecting one in the sun, she walked over to it and set down her bag. She picked up the towel, book, and suntan lotion that were supposedly claiming it and carried them to the deck boy. Sitting down, she slathered herself with suntan lotion. Then she lay back and opened her book, a romance set in the nineteenth century, about a sea voyage on which a fetching female passenger managed to captivate the surly captain and travel with him by sail all over the known world.

The sun was so hot that she quickly dozed off. She awoke, to find someone poking her shoulder. She looked up and saw a tattoo of a coiled snake running along the hairy forearm of the man who had awakened her.

"I'm sorry, madam, but you seem to have taken my chair." His ankle was wrapped in an Ace bandage, and he was balanced on crutches. A gimp. Tough luck for him.

"It's against the rules to save a chair if you aren't there to sit in it."

"I was only gone for a few minutes."

Glancing at her phone, Gail said, "You were gone for over an hour."

"Lady, if I weren't a gentleman, I'd hate to think what I might do to you."

"And if I weren't a lady, I'd charge you with assault for shaking my shoulder while I was sleeping."

"So where the hell is my stuff?"

Gail shrugged. "I gave it to the deck boy. He probably took it to the purser. That's what they do when someone tries to hog a chair he isn't using."

He glared at her with narrowed eyes. "Aren't you the same woman who pushed me down the steps on the top deck this morning?"

"I don't know what you're talking about." She fixed her eyes firmly on her novel.

JESSIE STUDIED THE LARGE TRIANGULAR BURN ON THE forearm of the woman in the pink tank top. "How did this happen?"

"I burned myself on an iron in the laundry room."

Jessie filled a basin with cool water and placed the woman's forearm in it. While it soaked, she retrieved some ointment and gauze. "Don't break the blisters if you can avoid it."

Jessie patted the arm dry and applied a thin coat of ointment and a loose bandage. "Elevate your arm and take ibuprofen for the pain. And stay away from that laundry room!"

The woman laughed. "With pleasure! My husband tells me that passengers who get into fights are thrown off the ship at the next port. Is that true?"

"So they say. I haven't seen it yet myself, but I've only been on this ship for a few days. Are you planning to fight with someone?"

"No, but I'd like to!"

JESSIE SAT BY HERSELF IN THE OFFICERS' DINING ROOM, eating *frutti di mare* over linguine. She could have gone to a guest dining room, but the first time she tried that, her badge reading

SHIP'S PHYSICIAN had betrayed her. Passengers had swarmed her and regaled her with the gruesome details of their endless ailments. She hadn't been able to eat a bite. So she had dined alone or with the nurses in this lounge ever since.

Ben came over carrying a plate of the linguine. "Mind if I join you?"

"Delighted."

He sat down in a bentwood armchair and unfolded his napkin. "There's a show tonight in the theater. Any interest in going with me?"

Jessie thought it over. Sitting alone in her tiny room with flashbacks to Kat's death, or sitting with Ben at a mediocre talent show? "Sure. Why not?"

After Ben and she had finished their decaf, they strolled along the carpeted corridor to the theater and found seats near the back so that either could slip out for an emergency at the clinic. Jessie enjoyed the high-kicking dancers and the Broadway show tunes, all somehow connected to a plot she couldn't quite grasp. But it was relaxing just to sit there and watch and listen, without having to take charge of anything. That was what she missed most by being a physician—passivity. People always looked to her for leadership in times of crisis, but sometimes she longed just to follow.

Kat would have loved this performance. She had adored all kinds of music, blues and country, folk and classical, gospel and rock and opera—everything except rap numbers with lyrics about raping and killing women. She had sung in choirs at church and at school as a girl, and had often broken into song around the condo in her off-key alto voice. She had played a baritone ukulele, poorly but with great fervor, often serenading their grandchildren with her signature rendition of "Froggy Went A-Courtin'."

Mona Paradiso, who, the program said, had been trained as an opera singer, came out in a form-hugging black gown and strappy heels. Around her neck was a silver collar with a green stone in the center. Jessie started. She had given Kat a collar just like that, from a silversmith in Provincetown, for her sixtieth birthday. Emerald had been her birthstone.

In a wondrous alto voice, the woman began singing a slow song Jessie didn't recognize. As she sang, the emotional pitch in the room began to rise. By the time she got to the chorus, the chronically aloof British were clapping in a startled flurry, not quite approving of themselves for showing so much uncynical enthusiasm. One man whistled weakly through his fingers. A few others called out timid encouragement, as though at a gospel revival of Anglo-Saxons.

The woman continued relentlessly:

> I knew someday
> That you would fly away
> For love's the greatest healer to be found
> So leave me if you need to,
> I will still remember
> Angel flying too close to the ground. . . .

Jessie pulled out her pager, pretended to check a message, and then whispered to Ben, "Sorry, gotta go."

He glanced at her, surprised, as she slid from her seat and raced out of the theater. Wrenching open the door to the walking deck and slipping through it, she grabbed the railing and doubled over in the balmy night air, gasping for breath while her heart raced. Her sign from Kat had arrived, delivered by that singer with the emerald birthstone at her throat.

Chapter 5

Wine-Dark Seas

JESSIE STOOD ON THE CREW DECK AT THE TOP OF THE SHIP.
Crew smokers on break were puffing away behind her. Like those
in the smoking sections on airplanes before they were banned,
these smokers were a loud and jolly bunch who seemed to be
having much more fun than nonsmokers. Apparently they were
choosing to lead foreshortened but hilariously cheerful lives.

Jessie was studying the ocean as intently as she had studied
Lake Champlain for the many years during which she and Kat
had lived on its shore. The lake had intrigued them both. They
used to discuss the wonders of water, the universal solvent, how
many crucial functions it served, from drinking to cleaning to
transport, how it could shift seamlessly from ice to mist to fog to
raindrops or snowflakes. They bought an old pontoon boat with
green vinyl seats and beige indoor/outdoor carpeting and floated
around the lake every chance they got, studying the interplay
among the water, winds, and clouds. They also endlessly dragged
grandchildren around it on inflatable rafts or water skis or boogie
boards.

The surface of this sea was equally fascinating, constantly
shifting from glassy to rippled to surging, from lapis lazuli to

cerulean to midnight blue. This afternoon the surface was as smooth as a mirror, disturbed only by the bulbous bow of the *Amphitrite* as it nosed its way through deep indigo water that reminded Jessie of a phrase from some distant Greek text that had never made much sense to her—"wine-dark seas." Wasn't wine purple? Weren't seas various shades of blue or green?

This very same observation had driven Kat crazy one summer afternoon as they sat sipping Sancerre on their deck overlooking Lake Champlain.

"Must you always be so literal?" she had demanded of Jessie.

"Yes, I must," Jessie had replied. "I'm a physician. If you had an appendicitis, how would you like it if I removed your ovary because it reminded me of your appendix?"

Kat had grown up in the South, that steamy green land of dreamers and fanatics. Coming north for college had been for her like a polar plunge. She spoke of the shock of seeing snow piled higher than people's heads along the Boston sidewalks, of hearing packed snow squeak underfoot as she walked, of feeling the sides of her nostrils freeze together as she inhaled. Life in the North was a serious business. If you weren't industrious in summer, you could freeze or starve in winter. The idle drifting and musing that entertained southerners would be a death sentence in Massachusetts or Vermont. Kat always used to say that the South had produced so many fiction writers because it was the only place in the nation where people could sit still long enough to write a novel.

The *Amphitrite* was now paralleling the coast of southern Oman. A row of sawtooth peaks and bare rounded summits separated the coast from the inland desert. Through her earbuds Jessie was listening to Willie Nelson sing "Angel Flying Too Close to the Ground," still trying to make sense of last night in the theater when Mona Paradiso had sung this song so powerfully that Jessie's overheated imagination had convinced her it was a message direct from Kat. Probably such goofy delusions were just a phase of the grieving process.

Jessie was unaccustomed to losing her head. It was a family tradition to become calm, cool, and efficient in the face of heightened emotion. She had first become aware of this phenomenon as a little girl. While visiting her grandparents in their antique brick farmhouse in rural Vermont, she had been stung by a bee. She began gasping for air. Instead of consoling her, her grandfather went quiet and appeared to withdraw into himself. Then he strode to the refrigerator, retrieved a syringe, and gave her a shot. Only once she was breathing normally again did he kiss her sting and paste a star-shaped Band-Aid on it.

But she had often witnessed in her father and in her brothers, who had also become physicians, this same detachment during crises, followed by rapid action. And she had had to develop that capacity herself in order to run her ER. So the knowledge that she had panicked and fled the theater when that woman was singing more than startled her. Could she be losing her edge?

She felt someone tapping her shoulder. Turning, she discovered Ben standing beside her in his officer whites. Reluctantly, she removed her earbuds and said, "Hey."

"Hey. Quite the view, huh?"

"Fantastic."

"See those mountains?"

Jessie nodded.

"The history of our species is being rewritten there right now."

"How so?"

"Archaeologists have unearthed some stone tools there that are over one hundred thousand years old, made in the same style as tools in Sudan from the same era. Which means that *Homo sapiens* left Africa earlier than anyone ever thought, and probably came to those mountains and spread north—rather than heading north into Asia and Europe through the Middle East."

Jessie looked at him. "I had no idea you were interested in such things, Ben."

"I was an archaeology major at Amherst. I never really wanted to be a doctor. I just did it to please my father."

"And did you?"

"Did I what?"

"Please your father?"

"No. He wanted me to be a surgeon, not an ER doc."

"So you might just as well have been an archaeologist and pleased yourself?"

He nodded with a rueful purse to his lips.

"How come I never knew this about you, Ben? After all, we did date for several months."

"I think we were always so busy at Roosevelt that none of us ever really knew each other. For instance, I never knew that you preferred to sleep with women."

"I didn't when we were together."

"When did you discover that you did?"

"Well, after you, I dated a few guys. I married one and gave birth to a son and a daughter, Anthony and Cady. Then I fell in love with a woman, and we had an important relationship for several years. After that ended, I dated a few more women. And then Kat came along, and we stayed together until she died. And now I'm nothing. So whatever that makes me is what I am."

"Bisexual?"

Jessie shrugged. "Maybe so. I certainly loved them all, at the time." She smiled.

"Good to know," murmured Ben. "Do you want to eat lunch with me, whoever you may be?"

"I'd like that."

After lunch, Jessie went down to the clinic for afternoon hours. She prescribed antibiotics for an Irishman's UTI. Then she phoned the purser to reinstate the room keys for several patients who had emerged from quarantine. The threat of a norovirus epidemic seemed to be receding.

She reflected on how much less exciting the *Amphitrite*'s clinic was than the Burlington ER. Is this what it would feel like to retire, suddenly having time to think about all the topics you'd avoided your whole life long? The average age of passengers must have been about sixty, so most of her cases now involved UTIs, constipation, seasickness, respiratory infections, and arthritis pain. Strokes and heart attacks would be something else again, but thankfully she hadn't confronted one of those yet. Nor had she seen the more dramatic injuries Ben described, those incurred by the young men belowdecks who enjoyed a wild nightlife and performed dangerous tasks in the engine room and on tall ladders around the decks.

A small older woman in a pink linen jacket arrived at the desk. "I'm afraid I've lost a tooth." She opened her hand to reveal a white porcelain crown on her palm.

"Lucky you didn't swallow it," said Jessie.

"It was a close call."

Jessie ushered her to the examining room and helped her up on the table. She shone a flashlight into the woman's mouth and located the stub where the cap belonged. "No problems that I can see. I can glue it back on for you."

"That would be wonderful," said the woman. "You're new here, aren't you?"

"Yes, I am. But how did you know that?"

"I live on this ship. I come to this clinic whenever I have a health issue. And you weren't here the last time I came."

"I just got on in Hong Kong. The doctor who was supposed to staff this clinic got sick himself. But you say you live on the ship?"

"Yes, I have a permanent cabin on deck six."

"So you just sail around and around the globe?"

"That's right. In return for my fare, I get all my meals, a place to live, transportation. It's more fun than assisted living—and it's actually cheaper, if you can believe it."

"Don't you get lonely?"

"Some of the staff are my friends by now. Interesting new guests from all over the world board at every major port. I work on sewing projects in my cabin. I take line-dancing lessons and exercise in the gym. My children and grandchildren get on at one port and off at another."

"Don't they worry about you?"

"They did at first, but I finally convinced them that this is how I want to live out my final years, rather than annoying them with my needs. Now they enjoy traveling to exotic places in order to check up on me."

Jessie put some glue into the cavity of the cap and said, "Open wide." She fit the cap on the stub and pressed down hard. "Don't eat or drink anything for several hours. And avoid chewy things like bagels or sticky toffee pudding for several days. You should be fine."

The woman hopped off the table.

"You've given me a lot to think about," said Jessie as she ushered the woman to the door.

"Stop by my cabin sometime for tea," suggested the woman. "Number six oh four two."

"Thanks, I will."

AT MIDNIGHT, GAIL SAVAGE LISTENED TO CHARLES'S STEADY breathing and concluded that he was soundly asleep. She slipped out of bed and donned her Gucci skinny jeans, Versace T-shirt, and ostrich-skin cowboy boots. In the bathroom, she brushed her hair and bunched it into a ponytail with a scrunchie. She put on some lipstick and eye shadow and liner. Gazing critically at her face in the mirror, she finally puckered her lips and blew herself an air kiss. So far, she had managed to keep the good looks that had earned her the title of Miss Florida Power and Light when she was sixteen. Once her looks were gone, though, she knew she was done for. Charles would probably be dead. She could collect a portion of his Social Security once she turned sixty. He had assigned her a life estate, which would allow her to live in their beachfront condo, and had made her beneficiary of an insurance policy. But he felt so guilty toward his first wife and their children that he had left everything else to them. They despised Gail for stealing their husband and father, so they would no doubt find a way to evict her from the condo. She had skipped college to marry Charles, and she had no skills, apart from seduction. She would probably wind up living on the streets. But meanwhile, she intended to enjoy herself as much as possible, like a midge dancing in the fading autumn sunlight. And if she happened to alight on a man who would save her from her future as a bag lady, so much the better.

Taking the elevator as far down into the belly of the ship as it would go, she emerged and looked around for the action. She could hear the thumping of an electric bass, so she followed it like jungle drums down the main corridor. Reaching the door to the crew bar, she drew a deep breath. Then she pushed open the door and strode in like a sheriff entering a barroom full of bandits. She was blasted by the sound of "Y.M.C.A." and the sight of several dozen bare-chested men forming letters in unison with their arms, like Dallas Cowboy cheerleaders. Gail plunged into the pulsing mass and started gesticulating along with them, while her neighboring dancers stared at her like stags encountering an albino hind.

When the song ended, many young men gathered around, offering to buy her a beer. She accepted this offer from a shirtless young man with a red bandanna headband, who had a nearly hairless chest and six-pack abs. When he returned with a Corona for her, his rivals faded away.

"Where did you swoop in from, beautiful lady?" he asked with a lazy smile.

"The tenth floor. Not much happening up there. I see now where all the action is!"

"Any action you might desire," he assured her.

At that moment Pedro, her room steward, appeared at her elbow, and Bandanna Boy moved aside. "You shouldn't be down here, Mrs. Savage."

She looked at him. "So who are you now, Pedro, my father?"

"It's not you I'm worried about, madam. It's these boys. They could lose their jobs for getting mixed up with a guest."

"Not my problem, Pedro. We've paid big bucks to be on this ship, and I'll go wherever I please."

"They're all supporting families back home," he explained in a voice that was almost pleading.

"Go to bed, Grandpa. Let us kids have our fun."

"Will it be fun when you and they get kicked off the ship at the next port?"

"We'll worry about that if it happens."

Pedro grabbed Bandanna Boy and spoke to him fiercely in Spanish. Gail grabbed his other arm and dragged him back to the scrum of dancers writhing away to the strains of Abba shrieking "Waterloo." Spotting the orange spikes on the head of Drago from the hair salon, she waved. He waved back deliriously. Then she whirled around and pressed her butt against Bandanna Boy's tight jeans, twitching it from side to side. Soon he was hunched over her, moving his hips in and out, while the other dancers cheered and whistled.

JESSIE SAT IN THE THEATER AT THE WEEKLY STAFF MEET-ing with those who weren't currently guiding the ship. The head of security, Major Thapa, a former Nepali Gurkha with the British army, was explaining why there had been such an upsurge in pirate attacks off the Somali coast in recent years. The major looked to be as short as Jessie, but with a neck as thick as a bull's. He was describing how fishing fleets from other countries had invaded Somali waters, depleting the fish population, on which Somali fishermen depended for their livelihoods. At first Somali "pirates" were merely angry fishermen trying to scare off these foreign ships. Eventually, though, Islamist terror groups discovered that they could capture large cargo ships and force their crews to operate them as "mother ships" on which pirates could live while prowling the seas in their small speedboats.

Captain Kilgore took over the podium as a map appeared on the movie screen behind him. With a laser beam he pointed out their current position at the head of the Gulf of Aden, with Yemen to the north and Somalia to the south. The ship would proceed along a banana-shaped path called the International Recommended Transit Corridor. The section of this corridor with the most frequent pirate attacks, known as "Pirate Alley," would be transited at night, when attacks were less frequent.

"But the most important thing," Captain Kilgore said, "is not to alarm our vacationing guests. With this goal in mind, we have removed the Tom Hanks movie *Captain Phillips* from the in-cabin TV selections. Just as a precaution, we will also stage a Safe Haven drill this afternoon so that everyone on board will understand the steps required from us all to safeguard our vessel in the very unlikely event of an attack. Staff and crew without other assignments are expected to participate as though they were passengers."

As Jessie and Ben exited the theater, she shot him an indignant glance. "How come you never mentioned pirates when you offered me this job?"

He smiled. "You might not have accepted it."

"You're damn right."

"Don't get excited. Pirates have attacked yachts and container ships. But they don't mess with cruise ships. Besides, there are all kinds of defenses in place that no one talks about."

"Like what?"

"How would I know? I told you that no one talks about them."

"Then how do you know that they even exist?"

"Rumors."

"Of what?"

"Of satellites overhead, and of submarines and warships nearby. Please don't worry, Jess. If we weren't absolutely safe, the cruise line would have altered the route. They can't afford lawsuits or bad word of mouth from unhappy passengers."

As Jessie descended to the clinic in the service elevator, she wondered whether she would have thought twice about signing on for this voyage if she'd known about the pirates. It was supposed to be a lighthearted lark, but it was beginning to sound more like her father's stories of dodging German U-boats on the North Atlantic during World War II. He had sailed on a British Merchant Navy vessel that was escorting a convoy of Liberty ships full of soldiers from New York Harbor. Every day he rode on an inflatable boat to a different troopship, clutching his medical bag, in order to give shots of penicillin to the hundreds of soldiers with syphilis. He said he had shuddered to think about loosing those hordes of diseased American men on the women of England and France. One night he had to perform an appendectomy using dinner forks as retractors, since no one had thought to equip the ship's clinic with medical instruments. While he sliced open his patient, his ship sent down depth charges against a swarm of U-boats below them. Afterward, he stood on deck as the sun rose and watched drowned German sailors surface amid the oil slicks from their destroyed submarines.

JESSIE SAT ON THE FLOOR IN THE HALLWAY OUTSIDE HER cabin for the pirate drill, her back against the wall. With one hand, she held the railing above her head. They had been instructed to close their curtains, lock balcony doors, and turn off the lights in their cabins. It was important to stay in the corridor away from the windows, and to hold the railing to avoid being thrown around the hallway if the ship had to perform evasive maneuvers.

Glancing to her right, Jessie discovered that her neighbor, sprawled in the corridor in torn jeans and a Broadway Cares T-shirt, was the woman who had sung so mesmerizingly the other night.

"Hi," called Jessie. "I guess we're neighbors."

"Yeah, looks like it."

"I loved that angel song you sang the other night."

"Thanks. I like it, too."

They sat in silence for a while. Jessie couldn't stop herself from glancing at the woman's scrambled auburn hair. Kat's had looked similar when she and Jessie had met. Kat had been several years older than she. Jessie had always admired the older Vermonters who had lived in communes and protested the Vietnam War and established food co-ops and free clinics and abortion centers. Jessie's peers had mostly sat around smoking pot and railing against monogamy. Jessie had asked for an autograph after Kat's reading from a novel at a local college. This had led to weekly lunches or dinners—and eventually to a romance so compelling that they had moved together into the condo on the lake. After their first decade, Kat's hair had become frosted with gray. By the time Kat died, her entire head had turned what they decided to call "fox silver." Now Jessie's hair had gone fox silver, too.

But the first thing she had noticed about Kat was her odd way of walking as she came onstage for her reading. Her toes pointed straight ahead, and she placed one foot directly in front of the other. It gave her narrow hips a fetching sway. Weeks later, once Jessie got up the nerve to ask her about it, Kat laughed and explained about her father's alleged Cherokee ancestor. As a child, she had read that Cherokees walked like that, almost pigeon-toed, so that they could fit their footprints into one another's on the warpath in order to conceal from enemies the number of warriors in their party. She had started copying that gait, and now she couldn't alter it.

"This pirate stuff is kinda creepy," said the singer, scooting closer to Jessie while still clutching the railing overhead.

"Yeah, who knew?"

"You've never cruised this route before?"

"I've never been on a cruise ship before," admitted Jessie. "This is my maiden voyage."

"No kidding? So what brings you on board?" The woman's New Jersey accent shared little of the rich timbre of her singing voice.

"I'm second-in-command at the clinic. I just got on in Hong Kong."

"Good to know I've got a doctor next door now."

Jessie laughed. "Just knock on the wall, and I'll make a house call."

"Let's hope I won't have to. But I guess norovirus is making the rounds these days?"

"I think it's about run its course. All we have to worry about now are pirate attacks."

"Can you believe that people pay big bucks to be chased around by pirates?"

"Nobody bothers to tell them about pirates when they're signing up. It's all about balmy sea breezes on your stateroom balcony and opulent souks overflowing with gold."

"The crew call the passengers Coneheads," said the woman, "after that family of aliens on *Saturday Night Live.* They remove their brains and leave them at home when they go on vacations. We must have all left our brains at home. But don't worry, they just do these drills to keep their insurance company happy. I've never even seen a pirate, and I'm on these ships all the time. It's how I pay my bills when I can't get a gig on land."

"Where did you get that beautiful silver collar you were wearing the other night?"

"I bought it at a silversmith's shop in Provincetown. I sometimes sing at clubs up there when I'm land-based."

The collars were a very distinctive design. Kat's had probably come from the same shop.

The ship's horn blasted several times to indicate that the drill had been completed. Jessie and her neighbor got to their feet.

"Nice talking to you," said Jessie.

"Likewise. My name's Mona, by the way. But I guess you figured that out from the playbill at the theater the other night?"

Jessie nodded. "I'm Jessie." They shook hands and returned to their neighboring rooms, Jessie somewhat unnerved. Apart from the auburn hair and the silver collar, Mona was tall and slender, very much like Kat at the same age—though she lacked the pigeon-toed Cherokee stride.

Chapter 6

Angel Gowns

JESSIE SAT UP IN BED. IT WAS HOPELESS. SHE COULDN'T sleep knowing that the ship might be running a gauntlet of mother ships. How sweet it was to know that young pirates rushed home to Mother after a busy day of seaborne depredation.

One snowy night as she and Kat were lying together on the sofa in their condo living room, watching the havoc on the nightly news, Kat had proposed that an uninhabited island somewhere be set aside for the young men of every nation. At age eighteen they would be sent there. Those who survived would be allowed to rejoin civilization at age twenty-five, once their brains had developed fully functioning prefrontal cortexes and their hearts had developed some compassion.

The men in their own families and those in the medical profession would, of course, be exempted. Jessie's grandfather had made house calls for decades in all kinds of awful weather to rescue rural Vermonters. Her father had spent World War II in French field hospitals, salvaging the lives and limbs of Germans and Allies alike. Her brother Stephen had served as a medic in Vietnam and now ran a team of physicians who staffed the huge sporting events in New York City. Her brother Caleb had founded a free clinic in Denver. Jessie had named her own son Anthony, after Susan B. Anthony. He had followed the family métier, like a Flying Wallenda, and was now working in the Burlington ER. Kat's father had joined the Freedom Riders and bore scars on his scalp to prove it. One of her younger brothers worked for the Southern Poverty Law Center. Her son Malcolm had founded a nonprofit that provided used cars to welfare recipients, and her son Martin ran a restaurant in Burlington that purchased most of its produce from local farmers.

But interviews with German soldiers after World War II had established that some had savored the destruction and suffering they had wrought. She wondered what factors made certain men healers and others killers. This was the great unanswered question.

Jessie's daughter, Cady, had been named after Elizabeth Cady Stanton, whom Jessie's mother had always claimed as a remote cousin. Cady was a social worker who defended foster children in court. Jessie was proud of both her children. They had sound hearts. They had also had to cope with a mother who had turned gay on them before it was fashionable. They had had to listen in silence as their teenage friends ridiculed dykes and faggots. And they had had to witness their mother behaving like a feckless teenager herself. Because Jessie had always been a dutiful daughter and a conscientious student, she didn't sow her wild oats until her thirties, when it was no longer appropriate, dashing from woman to woman like a crazed puppy chasing squirrels.

She shifted aside her curtain and looked out her window. It was dark and she couldn't see a thing, much less a mother ship full of angry young idiots. She removed her pajamas and pulled on jeans and a T-shirt. Surely the requirement that she wear her uniform in public spaces could be waived at 4:00 a.m.?

She walked to the service elevator and took it down to the fifth deck, where a few intrepid insomniacs were wandering the darkened hallways, frustrated to discover that the all-night buffet had been shuttered. Posted on the door to the walking deck was a notice saying it was closed until 8:00 a.m. Through the porthole in the door Jessie could see a security guard in body armor alongside the railing. His head was slowly swiveling, as though he were watching a beginners' tennis match. He appeared to be scouring the water for fast-moving motorboats. Beside him on a tripod stood what looked like a satellite dish.

Just then, Ben appeared in the hallway, dressed in a navy blue tracksuit. His heavy stubble, which used to be black, was now grizzled, frosting his dimples and the cleft in his chin. "You can't sleep, either?" he asked.

"It's too nerve-racking knowing that pirates might scale the side of our ship at any moment."

"No kidding. I was just doing the elliptical in the dark at the gym, trying to get too tired to care."

"Shall we await the dawn together?"

"Why not? The coffee machines at the buffet are probably working. Would you like a cup?"

"Sure. I have no hope of sleep tonight, in any case."

They sat on the starboard side at a window table with a drawn shade. Ben was cradling his cup between his hands. "I've been trying to imagine what this ship with all its bright lights would look like to a teenage boy in a pirate ship at night. It must be the embodiment of all his wet dreams—twenty-four-hour buffets, women in bikinis, and a bug-free bed. An earthly version of the Islamic paradise. And since he doesn't have the option of participating, he can at least try to destroy this embodiment of Crusader greed and lust."

Jessie nodded. "All these countries on the Gulf of Aden used to be important stops on the spice route from China and India to Egypt. The merchants transited this gulf in dhows packed with barrels of cinnamon and cardamom, ginger and pepper and turmeric, bales of silk, bundles of ebony and ivory, piles of exotic animal pelts, chests of precious stones and pearls. . . ."

She realized this panegyric was probably inspired by "Ithaca," which she had learned by heart for Kat's memorial service:

> *may you stop at Phoenician trading posts*
> *and there acquire the finest wares:*
> *mother-of-pearl and coral, amber and ebony,*
> *and heady perfumes of every kind. . . .*

How Kat would have loved this voyage. They had always discussed taking trips like this once they both retired. They had waited too long.

"So what happened?" asked Ben. "Why have they regressed to piracy?"

"Imperialism is what happened. Invasions by Egyptians, Assyrians, Persians, Greeks, Romans, Arab Muslims, Ottomans. And most recently, by the Portuguese, French, British, Turks, Italians. They all plundered the natural resources and exploited the cheap labor. They murdered anyone who objected or exported them as slaves. And then they went away, leaving those who survived the carnage to become enraged banditos."

"And an ER doc knows this how?

"I was a history major in college. Like you, I wasn't absolutely sure I wanted to be a physician."

Just then, the lights went on in the buffet area, and a server started opening the blinds. Once the shade covering Jessie and

Ben's window was raised, they could see the rising sun casting its crimson rays across the blackened water. In the distance, lights were winking from a harbor that sat inside what appeared to be the imploded crater of an extinct volcano.

"That's Aden," said Ben. "It used to be a British enclave. The USS *Cole* was bombed there by al-Qaeda in 2000 when it stopped off to refuel. Seventeen sailors were killed."

The barbed black peaks of the collapsed crater wall seemed to be gnawing at the gory red sky. A thick column of black smoke arose from the town center.

"Why doesn't the *Amphitrite* dock there?" asked Jessie.

"They're in the middle of a civil war. A Saudi-backed group is fighting an Iranian-backed group. The Saudis are Sunni and the Iranians are Shia, so that probably has something to do with it. But it's hard to keep track of who's doing what to whom over here, much less why."

He paused. "But I must say that you're very poetic this morning, Jessie. Exotic animal pelts and chests of precious stones! Danger must inspire poetry, because I wrote you a poem last night." He reached inside the pocket of his jacket, pulled out a folded sheet of yellow legal paper, and handed it to her.

Jessie unfolded the paper. She read a poem in his handwriting that appeared to be about the love he and she had shared in their youth, a love that still existed despite all that had intervened, a love that could rescue them both from despair in the present. Jessie was speechless.

He got up to leave. "I feel like a fool."

"Don't," she said, looking up. "I had no idea you have such talent, Ben."

"Think about it, Jessie."

"How could I not?"

As Ben walked away, Jessie just sat there. Kat had often recited poetry to her, until she had learned to more or less like it. Its vagaries were so different from her urgent tasks all day long at the ER. But she had to confess that it still remained like a foreign language to her. If this was really how Ben felt about their long-dead relationship, how could she refuse at least to consider rekindling it? However, memories of Kat still bound her like a shroud. And besides, she wasn't attracted to Ben anymore.

She picked up the poem and reread it. But what a poem! Could this be Kat's message to her from the other side, urging her to get on with her life? That would be just like Kat, to wish a man on her next, so that Kat's shade, if it existed, wouldn't have to feel jealous of a new woman.

AT THE CLINIC LATER THAT MORNING, JESSIE FOUND A note in her box from Iris Pendragon, the woman whose crown she had reglued. She invited Jessie to lunch in one of the guest dining rooms. Jessie phoned her, and they arranged to meet when Jessie's lunch hour began. Jessie was curious to hear more about living full-time on a ship. The concept had a certain appeal. This ship would arrive in Brooklyn in less than a month. Should she get off and go home to Vermont to refight battles she had already fought in her youth for birth control, abortion, environmental regulation, and world peace? Or was it the younger generation's job to defend these rights their parents had worked so hard to attain? Shouldn't they sign off Snapchat and get out in the streets? It would serve them right, all those young women who had sneered at feminists, if they lost access to birth control and abortion.

Should she sign another contract and keep working on the *Amphitrite* until she keeled over from exhaustion and they buried her at sea? Or rent a cabin and join Mrs. Pendragon as a permanent passenger? Moving constantly from place to place and person to person would be like practice for dying, when you had to leave everyone and everything familiar behind.

Alternatively, she and Kat used to talk about buying a yacht with their aging friends and putting it on automatic pilot out into the Indian Ocean east of South Africa, where Air Malaysia Flight 370 had vanished. They could socialize until they ran out of booze and then overdose on sleeping pills while the yacht crept like a Viking funerary ship along the blazing tangerine pathway laid down by the rising sun.

MRS. PENDRAGON WAS DRESSED IN BOOT-CUT JEANS, COWboy boots, and a plaid cotton shirt with mother-of-pearl snaps. She welcomed Jessie to her table by a window on the port side of the vast dining room that spanned the width of the ship. Jessie had removed her ship's physician badge so patients would leave her alone, but she still wore her whites, with medical epaulets that featured three gold stripes on a red background and a gold caduceus. It was like trying to camouflage a snow goose in a herd of Angus steers.

"Thank you so much for inviting me," said Jessie as she sat down.

"Thank you for accepting. I always enjoy getting to know the interesting people on board."

"I'm honored to be included in that category."

"But of course!"

"Is your crown okay?"

"Yes, it's been fine, thanks to you."

"What have you been up to since I saw you at the clinic?"

"Hiding from pirates in my hallway." Mrs. Pendragon laughed.

"Does this happen every time the ship transits this gulf?"

"Oh yes. From Muscat to the Red Sea is usually like this."

"Has this ship ever been attacked?"

"No, but they're smart to take precautions."

"Does it frighten you?"

"Not at all. The Lord is my shield and my cutlass!" She laughed merrily. "But how are you liking shipboard life?"

"I like it. But I'm looking forward to experiencing it without Safe Haven drills."

"Things will become much calmer once we reach the Red Sea, and we're almost there."

The tuxedoed waiter brought their salads.

"Do you mind if I say grace?"

Jessie shook her head, accustomed to these intimate meal-time chats with Jesus from her visits to Kat's family in North Carolina. According to the obituaries in the local newspaper down there, people in the South never died, they just went to be with the Lord. During grace, Kat's father had always referred to Jessie as "Kat's little friend." Afterward, he often announced that sending Kat north to college had been the biggest mistake of his life, since she had come back home a hippie. Jessie was pretty sure *hippie* was his code word for lesbian. Her mother had always assigned them separate bedrooms and had rattled on about which of Kat's high school boyfriends were still in town and still available. Jessie had been fascinated to watch Kat, queen of the barricades, meekly endure her parents' homophobic abuse. It no doubt explained why she had fled her homeland and rarely returned. It was strange that her father, so fierce in condemning racism, didn't hesitate to mock his daughter's choice of whom to love.

Mrs. Pendragon had lowered her head, closed her eyes, and was saying, "Lord, please accept my thanks for this delicious food, for this beautiful sunny day at sea, and for this wonderful new friend You have brought on board."

"Amen," Jessie said, to be amiable. "How are your line-dancing classes going?"

"I haven't been able to dance much the past few days. It seems every time I learn a new routine, I pull a new muscle."

"That's one of the joys of aging that no one ever warns you about," agreed Jessie. "But you said you have a sewing project to keep you busy?"

"Yes, evangelical women send me their old wedding dresses. My children bring them on board when they visit. I use the fabrics and the decorative lace and beads to make what I call my 'angel gowns.'"

"Angel gowns?"

"Yes, gowns for aborted fetuses and stillborn babies."

"Really?"

"I miscarried a baby myself sixty years ago. She was just dumped into a biohazard bag, and I never got a chance to say good-bye to her, much less to bury her."

"I'm sorry. How far along were you?"

"Three months."

"Uh, a three-month-old fetus couldn't very well wear a gown, could it?" She started wondering how to signal for Amy to summon her back to the clinic.

"I also make fabric envelopes decorated with lace and beads, for the fetuses too small to wear gowns—or tuxedos in the case of the boys."

"I see." Jessie realized Mrs. Pendragon's crown wasn't the only thing about her that had come unglued.

"Would you like to see some of my designs?"

While Jessie was wondering how to say no to a cruise guest without getting reprimanded by management, Mrs. Pendragon whipped out her iPhone and pulled up some photos. Jessie swiped through shot after shot of sad little withered creatures in miniature wedding dresses or tuxedos.

"So my outfits allow parents to give their babies a proper burial."

"I didn't realize cemeteries would bury fetuses, clothed or not."

"We have a law in Indiana stating that all fetuses must be either buried or cremated."

"You've got to be kidding."

"Don't you think that these poor little abandoned babies should be well dressed when they meet their Savior in heaven?"

"But fetuses aren't people yet, Mrs. Pendragon, at least in the judgment of the Supreme Court of the United States."

"But they are in the eyes of the Lord." She nodded knowingly.

Jessie always got nervous around those who believed they were channeling the Lord. "So once the fetuses are dressed in your outfits, will cemeteries bury them?"

"Some will. My husband, Don, who died several years ago, operated a whole-family cemetery in our Indiana hometown. He created a special section just for fetuses and stillborns and infants, with a brass plaque identifying it as BABYLAND. He also allowed puppies and kittens to be buried there."

Jessie glanced around, trying to locate the nearest exit. She pulled out her pager, pretended to look at it, and said, "I'm so sorry, Mrs. Pendragon, but I have an emergency in the clinic. I'll have to take a rain check for lunch."

"I didn't hear your pager beep." She eyed Jessie suspiciously, as though accustomed to losing her audience in mid-harangue.

"I felt it vibrate in my pocket."

"Well, I look forward to many more lunches with you, Jessie, as our cruise continues. And I thank the good Lord for bringing you on board and into my life."

Jessie smiled and nodded, reflecting that Mrs. Pendragon must not have yet figured out that her new pal was an enthusiastic abortion supporter. "Yes, it's been great fun, Mrs. Pendragon. I'll see you later."

As Jessie raced from the dining room, she began to feel angry. If you dressed aborted fetuses in wedding gowns and tuxes, it was to emphasize that they were little murdered people who should have been allowed to grow up and become brides and grooms. Even if you assumed this to be true, why did their needs trump those of the adult women who had unwittingly or unwillingly conceived them? Jessie thought about friends she knew before *Roe v. Wade* who had died from illegal abortions or from self-inflicted attempts to miscarry. She thought about the young girls she had treated in the ER, pregnant from being raped by uncles or neighbors. Young men died in war. Young women died in childbirth, or from trying to prevent it. Jessie had worked for much of her life so that her children and grandchildren would be spared both. But she had failed. Worldwide, a woman still died from an illegal abortion every seven minutes. And during the past 3,400 years only 8 percent of them had been war-free.

She drew a deep breath to calm herself. The sooner the Rapture occurred, the better. If all the fundamentalists of every persuasion got swept up to paradise, leaving behind only the heathens, this world might become a pleasant place.

Captain Kilgore was announcing over the PA that the harbor of Djibouti was off the port side. Once beyond it, the ship would pass through the Bab-el-Mandeb Strait into the Red Sea. To celebrate their uneventful passage through the pirate zone, a special Pirates' Tea Dance would be held on the main pool deck at 4:00 p.m. There would be free pirate-themed cocktails and a steel band!

Jessie went out on the walking deck to check out Djibouti. Concrete platforms seemed to float on the surface of the bay. On the platforms were the inevitable stacks of multicolored shipping containers. Orange, blue, and yellow cranes perched over the containers like Day-Glo praying mantises. Beyond the shoreline stretched low, arid gray mountains.

Jessie had kept busy on this cruise, dashing from port to starboard and back again, binoculars banging against her chest, in order to inspect all the sights on both sides. Ben had told her that the word *posh* had been coined by the British en route to and from India on ships around the Cape of Good Hope. It stood for "Port Out, Starboard Home." Passengers hiring those cabins could occasionally glimpse the lands they were passing by, rather than looking always at the endless sea. But for this reason, those cabins were more expensive, hence the term *posh*.

WHEN JESSIE ARRIVED AT THE POOL DECK, EVERY PERSON on board who wasn't working elsewhere appeared to be present. She and Ben were expected to put in appearances at these social functions when they weren't on clinic duty. The sky was bright blue, and the sun was beating down with tropical intensity. Some passengers had dressed as Captain Hook or Blackbeard, though most looked like Keith Richards on a bad day. Many still in swimsuits lay in lounge chairs, drinking cocktails with swizzle sticks shaped like tiny corsair swords.

Jessie spotted Charles Savage, released from norovirus quarantine, playing cards at a teak table with four other older men, all wearing blue baseball caps reading NAVAL VETERAN. Nearby sat Rodney Mullins, his bandaged foot propped on a stool. Beside him perched a woman with ramrod posture who clutched a beige handbag to her chest like a halfback protecting a football during a line drive. She seemed an unusually rigid mate for a man with a diamond-patterned snake tattoo winding up his forearm.

Jessie went over to the bar and ordered a drink called a Bacardí Buccaneer. As the band played in a dizzying array of musical styles, many passengers danced on the teak-floored pool deck. Iris Pendragon and a dozen others were bounding across it doing the Electric Slide, reversing directions in unison, like a school of fish. Sometimes they collided with other passengers, who were tangoing or mamboing. Somehow the setting for the Somali pirates had shifted from the Middle East to Texas and Argentina. It was as though the inhabitants of a nursing home had had their Ensures spiked with amphetamines. Clearly most had not been awake all night fretting about marine marauders.

Inexplicably, the steel band started playing "Memories" from *Cats.* Mona Paradiso was dressed as Tinker Bell, in a forest green bathing suit and a filmy green miniskirt with a jagged hem. A Sherwood Forest cap perched on her curly auburn hair, and she wore green spike heels. Small translucent wings extending from her shoulder blades quivered as she sang about the good old days, when life was beautiful and filled with happiness.

Jessie took a large gulp of her Bacardí and watched a gentlemen host wearing a navy blue blazer, white trousers, and a paisley ascot invite Gail Savage to dance. Gail was wearing white capris and a halter top that amply displayed her firm breasts and flat stomach. Her blond ponytail lashed as she and the host swirled across the deck in a swooping Viennese waltz. Many couples stopped dancing to move aside and make room for them. Rodney Mullins was watching Gail with what appeared to be a sneer.

Jessie spotted Ben in his officer whites standing near the band, seemingly transfixed by Mona in her winged forest green slut outfit. Mona was scanning the crowd as she sang. Once she spotted Jessie, she smiled faintly and nodded at her. Jessie waved back with her fingers.

As Gail Savage continued to circle the deck in the arms of the dapper host, Jessie spotted a young man in a blue jumpsuit lurking in a corner of the deck, studying the waltzers with a gaze full of menace. He wore a rolled red bandanna around his forehead. He was clearly a maintenance man, but what he was doing at the pool party was less clear. Maintenance men, like roaches, were never supposed to emerge from the belly of the ship in daylight.

Mona was singing relentlessly about the sunrise and the dawning of a new day and the determination not to give in to despair. Jessie took another hefty swig of her Bacardí and realized that she was getting sloshed. Blessedly, Mona was coming to the end of this song so crammed with lines that threatened pain for Jessie if she listened too closely.

As the crowd applauded, Mona bowed and backed away from the band. The band lurched into "Jamaican Farewell." A male singer, disguised as a castaway in bare feet and tattered cutoffs, seized the mike from Mona. Ben rushed up to Mona, and the next thing Jessie knew, Ben and Mona were cha-chaing back and forth by the steaming hot tub. So much for Ben's unquenchable devotion to herself, thought Jessie blearily.

A chef was carving a sculpture from a block of ice the size of a side-by-side refrigerator. Like a well-equipped torturer, he had an entire arsenal of tools—a chain saw, handsaws, hammer and chisels, a die grinder with an array of bits. He was working fast in the afternoon heat, and chips were flying in every direction. Jessie joined the onlookers so she wouldn't have to watch Ben and Mona's mating dance.

Setting down on a table what remained of her Bacardí, she watched the chef chip and drill and saw until gradually Johnny Depp emerged from the block of ice, incarnated as Jack Sparrow in a large tricorn hat. People began clapping as they recognized the distinctive face. Next the chef started hacking and scraping an untouched chunk of ice to one side of Johnny's head. Eventually everyone realized that it was turning into a parrot, one perched on Johnny's shoulder. They cheered and someone whistled. Another chef playfully placed a black eye patch over Jack Sparrow's left eye and stuck a dangling hoop near his earlobe.

Suddenly a glass panel under the starboard railing crumbled to the deck in tiny shards. A woman standing by the railing started screaming. A second panel shattered in place. Jessie could see a spiderweb of cracks emanating from a small hole through its center.

"Pirates!" several people yelled.

Some, thinking it a joke, started guffawing.

Jessie moved over to the railing and discovered that it was no joke. Two speedboats, each carrying a long extension ladder with hooks on top, were approaching the ship. Both boats held six young men wearing T-shirts and gym shorts. Most fondled AK-15s that were pointing skyward. A couple of them clutched what looked like either bassoons or grenade launchers.

"Everyone inside!" yelled an officer into the singer's microphone. "Repeat: Everyone inside! This is not a drill! Repeat: This is not a drill! This is a real attack. Everyone inside. Return to your cabins and perform the Safe Haven procedures!"

A mad scramble for the doors ensued. Jessie stayed put and watched the pirates several decks below her. They resembled her son, Anthony, and his motley pals when they were stoned in high school. Their battered boats maneuvered closer and closer to the side of the ship, boarding ladders extended well past their bows.

The next thing she knew, Gail Savage was helping the young maintenance man in the bandanna headband pick up a square teak table, scattering across the deck the stack of playing cards sitting on it. Together they tossed the table over the railing. It tumbled several stories down and grazed one of the boats, knocking an AK-15 into the sea. The pirates looked up, scowling. One raised a grenade launcher to his shoulder and fired wildly upward. The grenade exploded overhead. Meanwhile, Gail and the young man had each collapsed a deck chair and were hurling them over the railing onto the skiffs.

A security guard on the walking deck down below had uncoiled a fire hose and was blasting the boats with pressurized water when an extremely loud siren began to pulse and wail. The would-be pirates dropped their weapons to clutch at their ears. The mouths of a couple opened in silent screams.

Captain Kilgore came on the loudspeaker from the bridge. "Everyone inside now! Sit in the hallway opposite your cabin and hold tightly to the railing overhead as we exercise escape maneuvers!"

Gail and her friend threw one last table at the pirates and then raced for the door, as did Jessie. The engine roared as the ship accelerated.

"That was very brave of you," Jessie said to Gail as they pushed through the doorway side by side.

Gail shrugged. "Nobody is hijacking me!"

Jessie thought that if somebody did, he'd soon be begging her husband to take her back.

Jessie climbed the steps to her deck two at a time and careened down her hallway, past staff members sprawled on the carpet, clinging to their handrails overhead. She collapsed opposite her cabin and grabbed the railing as the ship cut through the water in a zigzag pattern that was no doubt throwing a huge crisscrossing wake that would swamp the small boats.

Mona, in her green bathing suit, was clutching the railing alongside Jessie. Her translucent wings were twisted out of shape. "There have to be easier ways to earn a living," she observed.

"Nice outfit."

Mona smiled. "Drago in the hair salon helped me assemble it. He says he knows all about fairies."

"Are we having fun yet?"

"I think we're okay. Those creeps can't board when we're going this fast."

"Did you ever hear of a Greek poet named Constantine Cavafy?" asked Jessie.

"Sure. 'Ithaca.' We studied him in high school."

"He wrote another poem, called 'Waiting for the Barbarians,' which I just read in a friend's journal. Some unidentified city-state is expecting an invasion of barbarians, and the officials are donning their ceremonial garb to greet them. But by the end of the afternoon it's announced that the barbarians aren't coming after all. The citizens become very agitated, and the last lines are 'And now what's to become of us without barbarians. Those people were a solution of a sort.'"

Mona laughed. "Yes, we may need our pirates. Otherwise, we might have to face the fact that we're pirates ourselves."

Jessie nodded. Mona was evidently bright and politically aware, as well as talented.

"Hey, can I ask you something about that doctor you work with—Ben?"

"Yeah, sure, what?"

"What's his deal anyhow?"

"What do you mean?"

"While we were dancing this afternoon, he told me he'd realized he couldn't live without me. I hardly know the guy, but he wrote me a poem." She handed Jessie a piece of paper.

On it were the opening lines of the love poem Ben said he had composed for Jessie. She started laughing.

"What's so funny?" asked Mona.

"He gave me the exact same poem this morning, supposedly written for me."

"Are you kidding me?"

Jessie fished her paper out of her pocket. Mona unfolded it, looked at it, and started laughing, too.

"You know what's even funnier?" asked Mona. "I studied French so I could sing French opera, and I recognize this poem. It's a translation of Jacques Prévert. Ben probably stole it off the Internet."

Jessie shook her head disbelievingly.

"I think we need to plan some revenge," said Mona.

"What do you have in mind?" asked Jessie warily. She enjoyed games with her grandchildren, but she was normally opposed to mind games with fellow adults. Still, Ben's duplicity did merit a riposte.

Chapter 7

The Flappers Ball

JESSIE AND MONA WERE SITTING AT A SMALL TABLE OUT-side a burger shack near the dog cages on the top deck. Mona was outlining her scheme to punish Ben for plagiarizing from Jacques Prévert. Jessie had spent the last couple of days dealing with injuries from the pirate attack—bruises and sprains as passengers had collided with one another while rushing inside from the pool deck, a couple of cuts from the shattered glass panel. Two people had fallen down stairs as they raced back to their cabins. One man had gone into atrial fibrillation. Others were tossed around their hallways during the ship's escape maneuvers. Nothing too serious, fortunately. Now they were halfway up the Red Sea, en route to the Suez Canal.

"Do you realize where we are?" Jessie asked Mona, to distract her from her lust for vengeance against Ben.

"It all looks the same to me. Water, water, everywhere."

"We're off the coast of what used to be called the Land of Punt. The Egyptian woman pharaoh Hatshepsut called it 'the Land of the Gods.'"

"It sure doesn't look very celestial now." They gazed at an arid plain that stretched down to the gray water. It was dotted with stunted shrubs.

"Well, apparently in 1500 B.C. it was a paradise. Hatshepsut sent a fleet of five ships here. They found villages of huts on stilts and vast groves of date palms. Also giraffes, leopards, and hippopotamuses. They carried home to Egypt baboons, ivory, gold, ebony, and shoots of trees with sap that yielded frankincense and myrrh. It's all depicted in bas-reliefs on Hatshepsut's mortuary temple."

"And you know this how?"

"I got interested in Punt in medical school. We were studying rare diseases that we would probably never see, and one was the Queen of Punt disease. The Queen of Punt was portrayed in the bas-reliefs as having massive thighs and buttocks and a malformed gait. It turns out she had a complex of conditions triggered by a DNA genotype that codes for lipomatosis, achondroplasia, lipodystrophy. . . ."

"I love it when you talk dirty to me," murmured Mona.

Jessie smiled. She was starting to like this woman. She was funny. If only people could just leave it at the laughter. It was once romance revved up that everyone's carefully caged demons came out to cavort.

"So we'll both write Ben a love poem stolen from the Internet," Mona continued relentlessly. "And we'll send them to him with notes saying that we're so enchanted with his poem to us that we want to pursue the relationship. Then we can sit back and watch him try to figure out how to juggle two willing women on one ship without either finding out about the other."

"You're really diabolical, Mona. Remind me never to get on your bad side."

"I seriously doubt that you could." Mona smiled at her. "Who's Amphitrite anyhow?"

"She was Poseidon's wife. Queen of the Seas. She used to be a very important goddess. She rode around in a chariot pulled by seahorses, wearing a fishnet and crab claws in her hair. But the Romans downgraded her to a sea nymph."

"How come a science nerd knows this stuff?"

"My partner of many years, Kat, was a writer. She forced me to read novels and poems, and to attend concerts and plays and art exhibits so I would be more well rounded."

"Past tense?"

"She died last year from esophageal cancer."

"Oh. I'm sorry."

"Thanks."

They sat in silence until Jessie asked, "What about you?"

"What about me?"

"Do you have a family? Children? A husband? A wife?"

"I have a huge Italian family in New Jersey. But no children or mate. I'm like a Vestal Virgin. I've devoted my life to my career. I keep an apartment in New York City, but I sing in recitals and with orchestras all over the country and abroad. My boyfriends and girlfriends have never stuck around, because I travel all the time."

Jessie nodded. "If Kat didn't go away when she felt the urge to write, she would turn snarky on me. But if she did leave and do her work, she came back home happy. So I learned to let her go. But I was so busy at the hospital that sometimes I scarcely noticed she was gone."

"Lucky Kat," murmured Mona. "A few times I got hired by the extra choruses at the Met. I applied for a full-time position with the permanent chorus, but I didn't make it. That would have been great, because those singers get a salary and benefits and a fixed work schedule. I could have led a normal life. Maybe had a spouse and some children. But I've had to face the fact that I'm not good enough."

"I think you have an amazing voice."

"Thanks. I know it's not bad. I was a child prodigy and sang all around New Jersey, at churches and county fairs and Moose lodges. I got a scholarship to Juilliard. But once you get to New York City, you encounter prodigies singing in every subway tunnel, trying to make a living. And now when I hear the really great divas sing, I know that I'm not in their league."

Jessie couldn't think of anything comforting to say. What did she know about opera?

"But it's okay," Mona continued. "I'll just keep on singing for whoever will hire me, until I lose my voice. It's not a bad life, doing what you love every day."

"Kat loved to write fiction, so she just kept on writing, even though many of her readers switched from novels to Netflix. She said it was like being a saddle maker after the invention of the automobile. But she also believed that if someone had a talent and didn't use it, something curdled inside them. Her publishers used to nag her about defining her brand. She'd say, 'What am I—a steer?' They advised her to establish a platform on social media, and she replied, 'If I blog and tweet, I won't have any time left to write fiction.'"

"It's definitely a new world out there," agreed Mona.

"I prefer the previous one, but I guess that's what old people always say."

"You aren't old."

"Yes, I am, and I've earned every single strand of this gray hair."

"It's not gray; it's silver," observed Mona. "Young women in New York City are paying hundreds of dollars to their stylists to achieve that color. It's stunning."

"Well, thanks!" Jessie had almost forgotten how pleasant it was to flirt, even if you were hors de combat.

GAIL SAVAGE TURNED AROUND TO INSPECT HER PROFILE IN the mirror on the closet door. Her new midnight blue backless gown, lifted from the laundry room, was perfect for the Flappers Ball tonight. It had a dropped waist with some tiers of fabric below. She was wearing white gloves that came above her elbows. Drago had bobbed her hair and shellacked a stiff curl from each of her sideburns. She had fashioned a headband from a wide golden ribbon. The captain, by way of apology for the interruption of the tea dance by the pirate attack, had announced this Flappers Ball yesterday. Passengers had been attending workshops today to prepare their costumes, borrowing items from the wardrobe room at the theater.

Charles came over and placed his white-gloved hands on her shoulders. "You look fantastic, my dear."

"Thank you, Charles. You look very handsome yourself." He did, too, in his tails with his white tie and white vest. Whatever his failings in bed, he looked superb in evening wear. In fact, the more she saw of Xander in his blue oil-stained jumpsuit, the more she appreciated Charles and his fastidious grooming. She wasn't quite sure what she had unleashed in Xander. Everywhere she went on the ship, he turned up with some tool for a chore he had invented so he could check up on her. Yesterday morning he had even come to her cabin to fix something on the TV that wasn't broken, so he could catch a glimpse of his competition—

even though she had repeatedly assured him that she would never leave Charles for him.

Still, as long as she and Xander were stuck on this ship together in the middle of the ocean with no way off, she had every intention of savoring his splendid physique and tireless libido. He had introduced her to places all over the ship where personnel took illicit partners for forbidden liaisons. The most exciting was atop the roof of a small elevator that ran from the library to the cocktail lounge. You got into the elevator, pushed the emergency stop button between decks, opened the hatch in the elevator ceiling, and climbed up onto the roof, where you found utter blackness and privacy for your exertions. Xander had stashed a blanket up there, so they were warm and cushioned. Her stifled moans probably made patrons believe the library was haunted. She also enjoyed their trysts in the compartment where the huge iron anchor and its chain were stowed. You could hear the ocean slapping the hull through the opening down below while you rocked in time to the heaving of the giant ship.

Xander claimed he had more hidey-holes to show her. Once she'd experienced them all, she thought she might end it with him. Curiosity was an aphrodisiac, but nothing could kill lust faster than repetition. And she saw no future with Xander, because he was as broke as she would be when Charles eventually died.

GAIL AND CHARLES STOOD IN THE DOORWAY OF THE BALL-room. On the dance floor hundreds of couples were struggling to do the Charleston while the ship listed and swayed. Gail clutched a gold mesh purse in one hand and Charles's arm in the other. The results of the outfit workshops were impressive. Many women wore ankle-length skirts and cloche hats, berets, or sun hats, plus fringed shawls or fur wraps. In keeping with the British tradition of bizarre women's hats, many were decorated with elaborate constructions from ribbons, pipe cleaners, netting, fake fruits and flowers, and stuffed birds. Some men were disguised as gangsters with spats and two-toned shoes, zoot suits, walking sticks, and homburg hats. Others wore tuxedos or tails, vests in clan plaids, top hats, and black patent-leather pumps.

A couple pushed impatiently past Charles and Gail, the woman speaking in a harsh Australian accent that sounded alarmingly familiar to Gail. The woman came to a stop and studied Gail. Gail noted the red triangular scab on her forearm and gazed quickly across the room.

"Hold on!" said the woman. "That's my frigging dress you're wearing, lady!"

The woman and her husband stepped forward until they were nose-to-nose with Charles and Gail. Gail stepped back and looked the woman up and down, as though inspecting a rabid raccoon.

Finally she said, "Prove it."

The woman opened her mouth, but no words came out. Eventually, she grabbed her husband's hand and they marched away.

A singer came onstage. She wore a gold turban with an ostrich feather waving above her head, and a sleeveless red flapper dress with lots of fringe around the hem. Some ropes of beads circled her neck. The orchestra started playing "Stardust."

"Let's dance, Charles." Gail dragged him toward the crowded floor.

THIS WOMAN IS GOING TO KILL ME, THOUGHT JESSIE AS Mona sang on and on about the pain of lost love, and music from years gone by that refused to fade away.

The beauty of her voice was devastating—to say nothing of the beauty of her person in her fringed red flapper dress and her sheer stockings with seams up the back. But Jessie knew it was important not to confuse someone's talent with the whole person. Kat had taught her that talent was an inexplicable gift from some higher source. But the person who embodied it was usually just an ordinary flawed mortal, probably a borderline psychotic if you really got to know her. Patients sometimes developed crushes on Jessie, assuming that her medical skills made her a superior person in every respect. When this misconception inspired them to make a pass at her, she usually thanked them for the compliment but reminded them that she awoke every morning with bad breath, just like everyone else.

This was one of those occasions when Jessie was grateful to be a medical officer. She was required to attend these passenger bacchanals in her uniform, so she didn't have to come up with a costume. She had, however, donned her white jacket and skirt in place of the slacks and shirt she usually wore at the clinic. She glanced at the Union Jacks that festooned the room. They seemed odd decorations for a Roaring Twenties party peopled with characters from Chicago speakeasies.

She spotted Ben moving toward her in his white dress uniform. Although she had declined to participate in Mona's plot to punish him for his faithlessness, she knew that Mona had shoved a love poem underneath his cabin door that afternoon. She wondered how he was going to react. The only thing she knew for sure was that she herself would never get into a bed with him ever again, in this world or the next. She only hoped that if he decided to focus on just one of them, it would be Mona. She certainly knew whom she would pick if she hadn't already deserted the playing field.

"She's amazing, isn't she?" Ben nodded toward Mona, who was now singing about spending lonely nights dreaming of a long-lost song that lingered in her memory.

"I'll say."

"Would you like to dance?"

"Why not?" She raised her arms to him. He took her hand and placed his other hand on the small of her back.

Mona was watching them as she sang. Her eyes met Jessie's and she winked. Mona's poem to Ben had been her own translation of "L'Hymne à l'amour," which Edith Piaf had composed for her lover, a French boxing champion, shortly before his death in a plane crash. Edith promised him that they would live together forever in the Great Beyond. Jessie wondered how that plan was working out for them.

She spotted the Savages. Charles looked dashing in his tails, with his perfectly parted silver hair, but his face appeared a bit green. Maybe he was seasick. She hoped he wasn't still incubating the norovirus. He was turning his wife over to a gentleman host who was dressed like Al Capone, minus the machine gun. Charles strode off the dance floor and headed toward an exit door.

Mona's song ended, and Captain Kilgore took over the microphone. A screen behind him lowered and filled with a billowing Union Jack, over which was superimposed an outline of the British Isles that looked very much like one of Mrs. Pendragon's withered fetuses. "We're so deeply happy to have you all here tonight, enjoying our amazing *Amphitrite* orchestra and our beautiful guest singer, brought to us direct from the Metropolitan Opera in New York City—Mona Paradiso! Let's give them a hand!"

The crowd applauded while Mona and the conductor bowed.

"You may be wondering about these Union Jacks decorating

our ballroom. We thought that after our little contretemps with brigands the other afternoon it would be fitting to remind you all of how safe our ship really is. And what better setting in which to do this than at a party to celebrate the 1920s? Need I remind you that at that time Britain held sway over a quarter of the world's population and a quarter of its landmass? Only twenty-two of the two hundred countries on the entire globe had not been civilized by the British. So we find it appropriate to mention these facts here in the Red Sea, which was entirely dominated then by the Royal Navy. No pirate would have dared attack a British vessel in those days—and in fact very few would dare it today. And as you have seen firsthand, those who do dare it fail miserably!"

Everyone cheered as the orchestra launched into "Rule, Britannia!" Mona finally had a chance to display her full operatic skills, as well as her fake British accent, as she trilled lines about Britain's emergence from the ocean at God's command.

The audience members not already standing leapt to their feet for the chorus, roaring in unison:

"Rule, Britannia! Britannia, rule the waves!

"Britons never, never, never shall be slaves!"

As Mona continued singing, the Brits shouted uncharacteristic encouragement to her and jumped up on teetering chairs. Many began frantically waving small Union Jacks on sticks.

Jessie felt her pager beeping in her pocket. Pulling it out and glancing at it, she turned and headed for the exit as Mona hit one of the highest notes Jessie had ever heard before, in a phrase having something to do with manly hearts guarding the fair. On her way out she spotted the same maintenance man in the red bandanna headband who had so courageously thrown tables overboard at the encroaching pirates. He was lurking by the doorway, holding a large wrench, staring at the delirious crowd howling about never being slaves. (Selling slaves, yes, but never themselves being slaves.) This young man was always turning up wherever Gail Savage was. Either he was stalking her or something was brewing between them.

On the phone out in the hallway, the operator on duty reported that someone had called 999 from room 10024 but that no one was on the line when she answered. Jessie recognized the room number as that of the Savages, and she recalled Charles's olive-tinged face as he left the ballroom. She assured the operator that she would follow up on it.

She pushed the elevator button for the tenth floor, and also the emergency button to prevent the elevator from stopping at intermediate floors. The medical team prided itself on arriving at any spot on the ship in two minutes or less. They had practiced this several times in Hong Kong after she boarded. But it was doubtful she would make it tonight, having had to thread her way across a dance floor packed with hyperventilating imperialists.

As she exited the elevator and raced down the hallway, an elderly couple came careening along in the opposite direction. The man, dressed in a tux with a Union Jack cummerbund, stopped, clicked his heels together, and saluted her. She saluted him back and dodged around his unsteady wife, who wore a mauve floor-length gown that revealed too much of her dimpled décolletage.

When Jessie knocked on the door of room 10024, no one answered. She opened the door with her master key. The room was dark and the drapes were drawn. On the king-size bed was a white comforter, on which Charles Savage lay supine, two foil-wrapped chocolate mints on the pillow beside his head. He didn't stir as Jessie entered. She went to his side and tapped his shoulder, saying in a loud voice, "Are you okay, Mr. Savage?" No response.

She flipped on the light. On the nightstand stood a pill bottle. Jessie picked it up and read the label. Viagra. The phone receiver lay on the floor. Jessie placed her fingertips on his carotid artery. No pulse. She lowered her face to his but felt no breath.

She did nothing for a long moment, withdrawing into herself and struggling to become calm and detached. Then she abruptly took out her pager and sent Ben a message, instructing him to call the purser to announce an Operation Bright Star, and to bring the crash cart to room 10024.

She quickly rearranged Charles's limbs, hiked up her skirt, and knelt over him on the bed. Locking her hands together and placing them just above the vee of his rib cage, she straightened her arms and began pushing on his chest in time to the lyrics of "Stayin' Alive" by the Bee Gees. After thirty compressions, she tilted up his chin and explored his mouth with her fingers for obstructions. She pinched shut his nose, locked her lips with his, and gave him two deep breaths. Then she returned to the compressions.

In the hallway she could hear the purser announcing quietly over the loudspeaker, "Operation Bright Star. Operation Bright Star. Guest deck ten, starboard side. Room one oh oh two four."

Jessie kept pumping away—press, release, press, release—to the throbbing disco beat of John Travolta's dance routine in *Saturday Night Fever*. She knew this procedure worked less than 10 percent of the time, but saving even one life seemed worth the exertion.

Soon the crash cart came careening through the door, with Amy and Ben close behind. While Amy gave Charles an injection, Ben set up the defibrillator. Then he tore open Charles's pleated dress shirt, studs flying all around the room. He applied the paddles to Charles's chest several times, but it was soon clear that Charles wasn't going to respond ever again. Ben, Amy, and Jessie fell silent and lowered their heads for a long moment.

"He has a wife on board," Jessie finally said. "I guess we need to find her." She picked up the phone and asked the purser to page Gail Savage and instruct her to go to the clinic as soon as possible.

The medical team plus Pedro, the Savages' cabin steward, slid Charles into a black zippered body bag and placed it on a stretcher. Officers had closed off either end of the hallway where the service elevator was located. Ben and Pedro carried the stretcher while Jessie pushed the crash cart.

Back at the clinic, Jessie and Ben pulled on latex gloves. Once they had removed Charles's evening clothes, Ben turned him on his side so Amy could snap some photos of the lividity that had already invaded his buttocks and back. Then Ben and Jessie coordinated like Olympic rowers to check every aspect of the cooling body. Their supervisors at Roosevelt would have been proud. Afterward they returned Charles to his body bag and moved it to one of the four slots in the refrigerated morgue.

"Do you ever run out of space?" Jessie asked as they closed the heavy door.

"Once we did. We had to get creative." He went over to the counter and started filling in the death certificate.

"Please don't tell me where you put the extra bodies."

The clinic door flew open. In marched Gail Savage in a navy blue silk backless gown. "Where's my husband?"

Jessie stepped forward. "Mrs. Savage, I'm afraid we have some bad news. Your husband suffered cardiac arrest. We weren't able to revive him."

"What?"

"I'm very sorry to have to tell you that your husband is deceased."

"Charles is dead?"

"I'm afraid so."

"Where is he?"

"In the morgue."

"A cruise ship has a morgue?"

Jessie nodded.

Just then, a woman in a dark blue skirted uniform entered. "Mrs. Savage, I'm so terribly sorry. My name is Eva Cummings. I'm from Guest Services. I can help you with the decisions and arrangements that will need to be made."

Gail nodded numbly. "When did this happen?"

"A couple of hours ago. We've been trying to page you, but we couldn't locate you," said Eva.

Jessie studied Gail's face for clues as to what she might have been up to that had prevented her from hearing repeated announcements all over the ship asking her to report to the clinic.

"I was visiting a friend," Gail murmured. "I didn't hear the page."

Eva offered Gail the British antidote to all tragedy—a cup of tea. Through the clinic porthole Jessie could see that the sky was taking on the tones of a boiled lobster shell. She was suddenly swept with exhaustion.

"Let's meet for a drink at the Naxos Bar tonight after dinner," said Ben as he and Jessie exited the clinic.

"Why not?" The little erotic game Mona and Ben had been playing suddenly seemed very silly.

"Good work last night, Jess."

"Thanks. That's why I'm here."

Jessie went up to the fifth floor and exited onto the walking deck. The rising sun was filling the entire sky with streaks of crimson, like an infected wound. Major Thapa was standing by the railing in his dress uniform, gazing through giant binoculars at the Nubian Desert of Sudan, which stretched right down to the seashore.

"Good morning, Major," said Jessie.

Thapa nodded at her. "How are you faring, Doctor?"

"Not too well, frankly. We just lost a guest to a heart attack."

"I'm sorry. I know you must feel as we do when we fail to foil a pirate attack." Major Thapa handed her his binoculars and pointed to the shore. "Take a look at the debris on that beach."

Jessie raised the binoculars and zeroed in on what looked like piles of branches, drenched in the bloodred dawn. But trees didn't grow in a desert. "I give up. What is it, Major?"

"Animal skeletons. Camels, wild goats, Barbary sheep, antelopes. Crossing the desert, they become crazed with thirst. They arrive at what they think is an oasis. They gorge on seawater and die of dehydration on the sand."

"But that's so sad."

He nodded. "Life in general is pretty sad, don't you think?"

"After the night I've just passed, I'd have to agree with you."

Back in her cabin, Jessie undressed and climbed into bed. Charles Savage's body was now chilling in the morgue. The force that had animated it had departed. Was this force still intact somewhere else, or had it dissipated into the stratosphere?

Kat's body had been cremated, reverting to the stardust from which it had been composed. This stardust now lay in Kat's ebony jewelry box on the mantel in their Vermont condo. Kat had asked for her ashes to be strewn across the shimmering waters of Lake Champlain, but Jessie hadn't yet been able to part with them. She needed to face up to that task so that Kat and she could both move on. But she didn't want to move on. She wanted to go back.

Chapter 8

Trios and Quartets

"HAVE YOU RECOVERED FROM OUR TRAUMATIC NIGHT?" Ben asked Jessie as they sat in comfy fabric chairs at a small round table in the Naxos Bar, overlooking the bow of the ship as it plowed through the waters of the Red Sea. Ben had kindly run the clinic all day long, dealing mostly with hangovers from the Flappers Ball and with sprains and bruises sustained by those who had fallen off the chairs they had clambered up onto while braying "Rule, Britannia!"

"I'm fine." Jessie removed the cherry on the swizzle stick of her manhattan with her front teeth. "I appreciate your concern, but I can't tell you how many deaths I've overseen recently. Mostly overdoses."

"It's different at sea. Sometimes the ship is so far out that even the coast guard and helicopters can't reach us to transport emergencies to land."

"Well, it's what we've been trained for."

"But it can still be unnerving when you recognize the reality. It's like being stuck back in the nineteenth century, with inadequate equipment and diagnostic tools."

"I can take it."

"I know you can. That's why I asked you to sign on for this job. You're one cool chick. I always used to admire your sangfroid at Roosevelt. It seemed to come naturally to you."

"It runs in my family. It's turning it off that has always been a challenge for me."

Ben nodded in agreement. "You were never an easy nut to crack!"

Jessie looked at him, hiding her annoyance at his possible implication that their failed relationship was solely her fault.

"Did you hear that the ship is skipping the Egyptian ports on the Red Sea and diverting to Aqaba, in Jordan, instead?" he asked.

"I heard, but I wasn't sure why."

"Too much political turmoil in Egypt since the ouster of Morsi. The Muslim Brotherhood is out for blood. The cruise line doesn't want to risk docking at Suez and sending passengers on buses to Cairo and Giza. They're offering excursions to Petra instead, which suits me fine, because there are some amazing digs going on there."

"Can I go to Petra, too, or do I need to run the clinic?"

"Hardly anyone turns up at the clinic on shore days, and there's a good hospital in Aqaba. So I think we can leave Amy in charge and both go to Petra."

"Tell me about these digs." Anything in order to sidestep a confrontation over plagiarized love poems. Jessie was regretting that she hadn't put a stop to Mona's half-baked vendetta. Just because Ben had behaved in bad faith was no reason for them to descend to his level.

"Well, Petra was the primary town for the Nabateans, an Arab tribe that controlled the land route from southern Arabia to Gaza, where frankincense and myrrh were shipped to Rome. It was carved out of cliffs of rose-colored limestone about the time of the birth of Christ. So the archaeologists at the dig sites are trying to work out how the carving was done so high up on cliffs with no evidence of scaffolding. And also how a city of thirty thousand people could have existed amid arid mountains with no water sources."

"And how could it?"

"They piped water from springs many miles away, and they constructed a series of sluices and dams to trap and store rainwater. They created an artificial oasis. It was a brilliant feat of engineering."

They were sitting in the rear corner of the lounge, right up against the wall. Apparently Ben was trying to conceal their rendezvous, presumably from Mona if she should show up there. Jessie knew for a fact that this would happen because she and Mona had already arranged it. A pianist was playing soft jazz, but Jessie could have sworn she had been hearing voices through the wall behind them. And now she heard rustlings and thuds. Could the ship be infested with rats?

"Do you hear that?" she asked Ben.

He paused to listen. Then he placed his ear against the wall. "Someone is having sex."

"Inside the wall?"

"I'm just telling you what I hear."

"Let's move. It's annoying." In his current state, Ben would probably eroticize anything.

Carrying their drinks, they shifted forward to another table.

"So what does the diversion from Suez mean for Mrs. Savage? I thought she was going to leave the ship there with her husband's body."

Gail Savage had moved from the room on the tenth deck where her husband had died to an empty suite the next deck up.

She was doing full Jackie Kennedy mourning in large sunglasses, a black head scarf with its ends knotted behind her neck, and dark draped garments that concealed her shapely physique. She had been spotted all over the ship, gazing silently out to sea over railings and through portholes, like the lead diva in a Fellini film. At the moment she was seated at a table across the room with a balding gentleman host, who was patting her hand while she wept, still wearing her sunglasses, even though the sun had long since set.

"That was the plan," replied Ben. "I called the medical officer on the Aqaba docks, but they don't have the facilities for her to disembark there. And Captain Kilgore doesn't want anyone to go ashore at Port Said, at the north end of the Suez Canal, for security reasons. So she'll have to wait for Alexandria."

"How long can her husband's body stay in the morgue?"

"A week, max. It's already been there for a day. But we'll reach Alexandria in four or five more days, so that should work out fine."

They both fell silent, feeling the presence of Charles Savage's chilled corpse eight decks below them, like an alligator in the sewers of Manhattan.

Just then, Mona arrived. She waved enthusiastically. Ben looked alarmed.

"Mind if I join you?"

"Delighted," said Jessie.

"Uh, sure." Ben stood up to pull over a spare chair from another table.

A waiter arrived and Mona ordered a mojito. "So what nefarious schemes are you two cooking up?"

"We were just talking about the trip to Petra tomorrow," said Jessie.

"I've always wanted to see Petra!"

"Why don't you come with us?" asked Jessie.

Both looked at Ben. He was studying his Rolex intently. "You probably don't want to be away from the ship for a full day," he said hopefully. "It's a two-hour bus ride over there. A two-mile hike down a canyon under a scorching sun. Two miles back out. Two hours back to the ship. I'm sure you must have important rehearsals."

"Nothing I can't get out of," Mona assured him.

Under the tiny table, Mona's knee brushed Jessie's. Jessie was annoyed to feel a frisson. Her unruly body had always had a mind of its own. Her brain had had to expend a lot of energy making it behave over the years.

"It'll be great!" Mona told Ben. "I can't wait!"

The three gamely matched one another drink for drink until Jessie realized she would never make it to the bus in the morning if she didn't stop. She excused herself and left Mona to cope with an increasingly disgruntled Ben, who had evidently never experienced the delights of an equilateral triangle. He seemed unaccustomed to not being the sole focus of every woman's attention.

THE *AMPHITRITE* PASSENGERS ON THE AQABA QUAY MILLED around, searching for their buses. Some were going to stay overnight in Louis Vuitton tents and share a feast of roasted camel calves with a tribe of bewildered Bedouins. Others were riding camels to sites around Aqaba associated with Lawrence of Arabia's skirmishes with the Ottomans, prior to his capture and rape in their jail.

Ben, Jessie, and Mona finally located their bus to Petra. Mona and Jessie sat together, while Ben sat behind them in glum silence. They passed guidebooks back and forth and snapped iPhone photos out the window of Bedouin encampments of black tents and vast herds of woolly sheep.

After emerging from the bus into a parking lot, the three walked side by side down a narrow limestone chute, a fissure formed by an ancient earthquake. The rose-tan-and-gray-striated walls on either side loomed so high that they blocked out the sky, turning the passageway dim and shadowy. They stopped to inspect low ledges along the walls. Ben pointed out the declivities in them that had once contained clay pipes to conduct water from distant springs.

A rickety old carriage with a black leather hood careened past them, drawn by a gaunt horse with prominent ribs. A young man in Arab headgear was flogging it with a riding crop.

The elderly British woman passenger was calling, "Young man! Young man! Stop mistreating that horse this instant, or I promise you I will climb down and walk! Without paying your fare, mind you!"

The carriage with its flapping leather hood hurtled on past them down the canyon, scattering pedestrians like pigeons before a peregrine falcon.

At last the three rounded a curve in the path, and there before them, carved into a cliffside of rose limestone several hundred feet high, was a façade with giant pillars, pediments, and cornices that featured a bizarre mélange of Greek, Roman, and Egyptian details. They stood completely still, stunned by the enormity, magnificence, and incongruity of the structure.

Another kamikaze carriage appeared behind them, the clattering of the horse's hooves echoing throughout the ravine. Dodging out of its trajectory, they continued their stunned inspection of the building that guidebooks labeled "the Treasury."

Finally turning right and continuing down the pathway that Ben said had been the main street, they reached a small amphitheater carved into another cliff of rose limestone. On rocky ledges around the amphitheater perched small templelike buildings with ornate Greco-Roman doorways.

"What are those?" Jessie asked Ben.

"Tombs."

"They scattered their tombs up and down the main street of town?"

"The ancient Arabs didn't quarantine the dead from the living as we do."

He pointed out a central plaza where pools, canals, and groves of date palms had once flourished. The Nabateans had maintained their artificial oasis for several centuries. Now it had reverted to a parched and rocky wasteland.

"What the hell happened to this town?" asked Jessie.

"The usual," said Ben. "Invasions by Romans, Persians, Arabs. Earthquakes and floods."

While Ben clambered around the cliffs, inspecting what was left of the hydraulic system and chatting with the archaeologists, Mona and Jessie climbed up to one of the small tombs and ducked inside. The stone floor and walls were completely bare, but a forest of freestanding pillars of striped limestone supported the ceiling. Many coffin-size niches had been hollowed into the walls. Grave robbers or archaeologists must have long since plundered any skeletons or grave goods.

It was cool and dark there, so they sat down on the ground by the doorway and gazed out at the merciless desert sun baking the swarms of tourists wandering amid the arid debris of the once-green and prosperous town.

"I think my plan to torture Ben isn't working," announced Mona.

"Has he said anything to you about your note or poem?"

"No. But at least it may have stopped him in his tracks. He doesn't seem to know what to do with us both at once."

Jessie nodded wearily. What was this—middle school? They sat in silence while the hum of the more conscientious tourists rose up from the valley floor.

"I always think of other people in terms of pieces of music. Do you know which you remind me of?" asked Mona.

"Which?"

"Haydn's String Quartet number ten in A Major."

"Sorry, but I don't know it."

"See if you can find it on YouTube when we get back. It's definitely you. It exudes a quietly contained passion."

Jessie couldn't think of anything to say in response. Thank you? But Mona's remark sounded like a line she might have used on someone else—a line that had probably already worked on someone else.

"Thanks, I'll check it out," Jessie finally replied.

Ben eventually came to retrieve them, and they struggled back up the narrow stone gorge, in and out of the sunlight, dodging the lurching carriages, until they arrived at their bus. As they boarded, Ben managed to slip into the seat beside Mona. That worked fine for Jessie. She dozed while Ben regaled Mona with the entire archaeological history of the Arabian Peninsula.

Back at the ship, they went their separate ways—or at least Jessie presumed they did. In any case, Jessie went to her cabin and located the Haydn quartet on YouTube. Listening to it, she was quite perplexed. It was a gorgeous piece, calm and soothing.

Anyone would have been flattered to be compared to it. So what was Mona Paradiso up to now? All she wanted, Jessie told herself, was to mourn Kat in peace.

The Internet was suddenly working well, so her e-mails that had accumulated during the days at sea downloaded all at once. Cady wrote about one of her foster children, who was having sex with her foster brother. She attached a drawing her daughter Maya had done at kindergarten of Jessie, dressed in scrubs, with a purple stethoscope around her neck, standing atop a ship surrounded by water full of colorful fish. Anthony brought her up-to-date on personnel problems at the Burlington ER. Martin wrote about difficulties with some organic suppliers for his farm-to-table restaurant. Malcolm's son had underperformed on his ACTs. On and on it went. Together, she and Kat had dealt with their children's and grandchildren's issues. Alone, Jessie doubted she could do it anymore. She had journeyed to the underworld and back three times during the last two years. She was half-dead herself. She had nothing left to give.

Another e-mail appeared, from Louise, Kat's best friend, an English professor at the University of Vermont: "Are you okay, Jessie? I saw Anthony the other day at the Fresh Market, and he said you're on a cruise in the Red Sea. WTF? We've all been worried about you. You left so abruptly, and no one has heard from you since. When are you coming back home?"

Louise was also a poet. Kat and she had attended many poetry readings together. They had also met often to critique each other's poems. Jessie had been jealous of this relationship at first, since Louise offered Kat things that Jessie couldn't. But Kat had pointed out that Jessie had colleagues at the ER with whom she could discuss her cases. Whereas Kat worked alone all the time, having as company only her characters, who functioned for her rather like imaginary playmates for a lonesome child. But she, too, needed actual colleagues with whom to discuss her work.

Jessie felt a stab of guilt. She had sometimes been very selfish. Kat had sat at her desk in silence all day long. At night she had wanted to talk. But Jessie had talked all day long, so at night she had wanted silence.

Jessie hesitated and then decided not to answer Louise. She didn't know how to explain her sudden impulse to get away from anyone and anything that could remind her of Kat. And she didn't know how to answer the question of when she would return to Vermont because she wasn't even sure she would. Some days she longed for a fresh start in a new place with people who had never known Kat.

She removed Kat's notebook from the drawer of her bedside table and started reading where she had left off. Kat was clearly planning to write another novel, but what about? To Jessie's surprise, she came to some notes about Alexandria, Egypt, where the *Amphitrite* would dock in a few days. In addition to information about Alexandria's history and landmarks, Kat had copied out several more Cavafy poems. Cavafy had evidently been born there and had lived there for most of his life.

There were also notes about Alexander the Great, who had founded the city. About Cleopatra, whose palace had been located beside the harbor there. About E. M. Forster, who apparently experienced his first serious love affair with a man there during World War I. About Marguerite Yourcenar, who had written a novel featuring Hadrian, whose handsome young boyfriend had drowned himself in the Nile not far from Alexandria.

Jessie hadn't known the *Amphitrite* would dock at Alexandria when she signed on for this job, nor had she known that Kat had been preoccupied with the city during her final months. This was one of those serendipitous moments when the universe alerts you to the fact that life on this Earth has complex dimensions that are hidden from you—and will probably remain so.

Jessie was mystified. What in the world did Alexandria, Egypt, have to do with Kat Justice from Mink Ridge, North Carolina? It was unnerving to realize that, although she had caressed every square inch of Kat's body many hundreds of times, there were evidently levels on which Kat had been a stranger to her.

Chapter 9

Puffer Fish

JESSIE WAS SITTING ALONE AT A TABLE IN THE OFFICERS' dining room, eating scrambled eggs on toast. The *Amphitrite* was at anchor, waiting to pass through the Suez Canal. At the next table sat James Yancey, a junior officer from the bridge, earnest and clean-cut in his natty white uniform with his buzz-cut hair, like an escapee from a Mormon door-to-door proselytizing team. He and she had once compared iPhone photos of her grandchildren in Vermont and his fiancée back home in Lyme Regis. Across from him sat Major Thapa. Jessie had been listening to their conversation concerning Thapa's childhood in Nepal. He had won one of the coveted spots as a Gurkha, out of thirty thousand applicants, by running uphill for forty minutes with a wicker basket full of seventy pounds of rocks on his back.

"Gosh," said James, "I could never have made Gurkha, that's for certain!"

"It's an important tradition in my family. We used to belong to the warrior caste back in the bad old days. Many ancestors and relatives before me fought for Britain in India, Malaya, Burma, Borneo, Tibet, the Falklands, Kuwait, Kosovo, you name it."

"Where did you serve before the *Amphitrite*?"

"I fought the Taliban in the mountains of Afghanistan. That's where I learned to think like a snake. That's the whole secret to my job—imagining the most devious and perverted things anyone never thought of, and then trying to prevent them. But we certainly fell down on the job the other day with those pirates."

"Sounds hair-raising."

"Yes, I'm a nervous wreck most of the time, pretending I can foresee the unforeseeable." He unwrapped an antacid tablet and popped it into his mouth, as though to prove his point.

"What worries you most right now?"

"Where do I start? Rocket-propelled grenades or missiles launched from the banks of the canal. A fishing boat crammed with explosives ramming our hull. A bus carrying our guests on a field trip being attacked, as happened at that museum in Tunis not long ago. Terrorists disguised as crew taking over the ship, as they did the *Achille Lauro* when it docked at Port Said in 1985."

"Okay, that's enough!" James laughed nervously.

"The motto of the Gurkhas is 'Better to die than to be a coward.' What I object to most about these Islamists is that they kill unarmed civilians by stealth. That's cowardly. Yet they think of themselves as Davids facing down the Goliath of Crusader civilization. But David was armed with nothing but a slingshot. If you want to be a hero, prevail over someone who's at least as well armed and forewarned as you yourself are."

Jessie leaned over and said, "I apologize. I was eavesdropping just now. I must say I'm a bit startled. I had thought we were home free now that we're out of the pirate zone."

Thapa said, "I'm afraid the *Amphitrite* is never home free, Doctor. Can you imagine what a coup it would be for those young thugs to sink this amazing ship?"

"I guess you're right. Well, thanks for watching out for us, anyhow, Major."

"My team and I are trying our best to keep everyone safe. Just as I know you and your medical unit are doing."

"Would you like to come up on the bridge and watch us navigate the canal, Doctor?" James asked.

"Wow, I'd love to!"

"The only requirement is that no one talk, because our officers have to concentrate very hard in order to avoid collisions, with these huge ships so close to one another. It's like a parade of whales."

"I can do that," Jessie assured him.

JESSIE STOOD SILENTLY IN A CORNER ON THE BRIDGE WHILE Captain Kilgore, James, several other officers, and a local Egyptian pilot oversaw a vast dashboard of screens, dials, switches, and levers. Two of Major Thapa's men were at the windows, gazing in every direction through huge binoculars.

Raising her own binoculars, Jessie inspected the ships anchored near the canal entrance—another cruise ship with many decks of cabins and balconies, like a top-heavy hotel; a cargo ship, its multicolored containers of Chinese designer knockoffs stacked as tightly as a Rubik's Cube; a commercial fishing trawler with hoists and nets; an empty car carrier, a private yacht, a petroleum tanker, two Chinese gunboats. The exposed hulls of the large ships were painted rust, turquoise, peacock blue, or jade green. The colors were vibrant against the grays and tans of the murky water and the shores of baked sand.

Despite what James had told her about the need for silence,

Captain Kilgore was talking quietly to Major Thapa, explaining that the wait time for entering the canal had recently been reduced from ten hours to three because a side channel had been excavated south of Port Said to allow ships to travel in both directions at once, rather than having to take turns through the narrow sections. A hundred ships a day could now transit the canal, as opposed to fifty before. But because the price of oil had fallen so low, some tankers were taking the longer route to Europe and the United States around the Cape of Good Hope, rather than pay the $450,000 toll to Egypt to pass through the canal.

"What will this do to the Egyptian economy?" asked Major Thapa.

"I think the whole Middle East will eventually implode," said Captain Kilgore, "as oil continues to be replaced by renewable energy. Countries that have luxuriated in their oil wealth will have to diversify. It's ironic, but the source of their past wealth—the oil—is what's causing the global warming that's rendering their home countries uninhabitable, outside of air-conditioned buildings. They're having more and more days that reach forty degrees centigrade. At that temperature, sweat won't evaporate, so laborers can no longer work outdoors on oil rigs and construction projects. Pilgrims may not be able to go on the hajj. There's no telling what could happen in Mecca with two million people exposed to a couple of forty-degree-centigrade days. It's a recipe for mass heatstroke.

"Of course, eventually Russia, Canada, and the Scandinavian nations will probably emerge as the dominant world powers because so much of their landmass is in the Arctic, which will thaw and become habitable—with the natural resources exploitable."

Jessie was surprised to hear Captain Kilgore sounding so

sober, accustomed as she was to his breezy noontime paeans to life at sea. But what most surprised her as the ship inched into the canal was how shallow and narrow it seemed. Eighty-some feet deep and less than two football fields wide, James had told her. It was actually just a big ditch dug through the sand dunes, with no locks or quays. On the eastern side stretched the Sinai desert, whereas the western side was more verdant, thanks to water siphoned from the Nile.

The *Amphitrite* floated slowly but inexorably past the city of Suez, like a Hindu juggernaut that would grind any devotee in its path beneath its implacable wheels. Beyond the Suez docks, two minarets pierced the cerulean sky, where puffs of white cloud floated lazily. On the far outskirts of the city, two young men in red-and-white-checked kaffiyehs lounged on the backs of camels to watch the huge boat drift past. After hearing Major Thapa itemize the varieties of attacks that were possible, it first occurred to Jessie to be afraid of these handsome, dark-eyed, white-teethed desert boys. But she nevertheless snapped some photos of them with her iPhone to text to her grandchildren.

The canal appeared well protected. Staffed guard towers like giant mushrooms were planted at regular intervals on either bank. Jeeps full of armed Egyptian soldiers were parked at every ferry crossing. Partway up the canal they came to a military base with a large barracks surrounded by some covered trucks packed with soldiers.

Near midday they reached Ismailia, where the Egyptian pilot descended from the bridge and swung off the *Amphitrite* onto a waiting tugboat. Another pilot grabbed the ladder and scaled the side of the ship, soon appearing on the bridge to shake hands with Captain Kilgore. Outside, the eerie call to prayer emanated from several competing minarets.

Once the call had ended, Captain Kilgore switched on the PA system and launched into his lunchtime encomium: "I hope you're all enjoying our little jaunt up the Suez Canal toward the Mediterranean. Just to give you some background: The Egyptians as early as 1800 B.C. dug canals from the Nile River to lakes that have been incorporated into this canal. Even then this was an important trade route from India and China, Arabia and East Africa, up the Red Sea to Egypt and the Mediterranean. But no one ever tried to join the Red Sea to the Mediterranean directly because they believed that the two bodies of water were of different heights and that one would flood the other.

"A French engineer named Ferdinand de Lesseps established that this was not the case and began our current canal in 1859 with financial backing from the British. It took ten years and one hundred and twenty thousand Egyptian lives to dig this one-hundred-and-seventy-kilometer-long canal. European ships traveling to and from the East used to have to circle the Cape of Good Hope. This canal saved them three weeks and seventy-two hundred kilometers.

"To acknowledge the importance of the British contribution to the construction of this canal, a British ship, the HMS *Newport,* led the flotilla during ceremonies on its opening day."

Jessie could hear passengers cheering as they leaned off their balconies, waving their Union Jacks on sticks. Some warbled "Rule, Britannia!"

James left the banks of screens and dials to come stand beside her.

"Thanks," she whispered. "This is amazing."

He nodded.

Up ahead a small fishing boat being rowed by a teenage boy lay directly in their path. The pilot boat escorting their twelve-story leviathan rushed forward and started nosing the craft toward the western shore. A second fisherman in the small craft, clad in only a loincloth, hurriedly gathered in tangled armloads of wet nets. As the *Amphitrite* passed him, he stood up on the rear seat of his rowboat and raised high what looked like a trident. On it was impaled a creature that resembled an albino basketball bristling with spikes. He shook it at the *Amphitrite,* his face contorted with what appeared to be rage.

"Gosh, what's that monstrosity?" she whispered to James.

"It's a puffer fish. They're invading the Mediterranean from the Red Sea via this canal. They contain a toxin twelve hundred times more poisonous than cyanide. One fish could paralyze the respiratory systems of thirty swimmers, and there's no antidote."

"What will nature dream up next?"

"I know. It's really grotesque."

"Is that gorgeous boy threatening us with his poison fish?"

"Sure looks like it to me."

"Remind me not to eat any more sushi."

James laughed.

"You know, I never realized that this trip would become so sinister. When I signed on, I was thinking more along the lines of the Love Boat."

"It's both, Doctor. Love and death. Eros warring with Thanatos, just like Freud said."

Jessie looked at James speculatively. She hadn't pegged him as someone who would be interested in the contradictions of the psyche.

Jessie took her leave to go run the afternoon clinic. She arrived just as Ben was departing. He greeted her without enthusiasm. This seemed odd, since he was supposedly trying to resuscitate their long-dead romance. Had he figured out that she wasn't

interested? Or had he Googled Mona's poem and discovered that
it was penned by Piaf? Did he only relish the chase, losing interest once his prey had acquiesced? Or was he just in a bad mood
because of the injustice of his being required to support his harem
of ex-wives and their children?

Who knew? Who cared? Certainly not she. She smiled at
him, grabbed a stack of patient questionnaires, and retreated to
her office. On her desk was a phone message from Mona inviting
her for a drink in the Naxos Bar that evening. She left Mona a
phone message accepting and then called Amy to request the next
patient, who was in agony from an ingrown toenail.

WHEN JESSIE WALKED INTO THE NAXOS BAR, SHE SPOTTED
Mona at a small table, chatting with a couple of guests. Once
she reached them, she discovered they were all speaking French.

Mona introduced her to Veronique and Pascal Vincent. "The
Vincents are annoyed by Captain Kilgore's version at lunchtime
today of the construction of the canal."

They nodded fiercely. "The French built this canal!" exclaimed
Pascal, switching to English for Jessie's benefit. "The British
refused to help finance De Lesseps. They didn't want competition
for their ports on the Cape of Good Hope route to India. Once
it became apparent the canal would prove a success, the British
bought up some Egyptian shares. But the French always owned
the majority interest."

Veronique, swathed in a scarf the size of a bridge tablecloth
from the Hermès boutique, joined him in his outrage: "Yes, and
at the opening ceremony, the Egyptian pasha and the empress
Eugénie of France were slated to go first down the canal in the
imperial yacht *L'Aigle,* piloted by a Frenchman. But the night

before, that British ship turned off its running lights and wove among the anchored vessels until it was first in line, blocking *L'Aigle* and taking the lead."

"*Encore une fois, la perfide Albion!*" snarled Pascal.

"We know all about the wiles of the British where I come from," agreed Jessie, speculating that Veronique's giant scarf could be pitched as a pup tent should she get lost in the desert.

"And where is this?" asked Veronique.

"New England. The Boston Tea Party and Paul Revere and all that."

"And Lafayette?" suggested Pascal.

"Yes, we do appreciate your sending us Lafayette," said Mona.

"What do you mean 'we'?" asked Jessie. "You're Italian. I bet your family didn't even arrive in the States until the twentieth century?"

"That's true," said Mona.

They all laughed as the Vincents stood up. "You don't need to leave," said Jessie.

"We want to go out on deck to see Port Said."

After the Vincents had departed, Jessie said, "Boy, the British and the French have really got it in for each other, don't they?"

"They don't really," said Mona. "Despite all their wars back and forth, the British love French food and wine. And the French love British tweeds and plaids. But how have you been, Jessie?"

"Great! I was on the bridge all morning."

"I missed most of the transit. I had to rehearse our new production for hours. The male lead is a real loser. His previous experience consists of playing Goofy at Disneyland."

"You must be exhausted if you danced all day."

"Yeah, I am. By the way, did you find that Haydn piece on YouTube?"

"Yes. It was really lovely."

"Did you see what I mean about its suiting you?"

"Well, I'm flattered that you think so, Mona. But I should warn you that I can be just as stressed-out as anyone else."

Mona smiled tightly. "And just as unable to accept a compliment?"

"I accept it with thanks. But I also think that you don't know me very well."

"Yet."

Jessie smiled and nodded. "Yet."

"Any new developments with our perfidious boyfriend?" inquired Mona.

"I saw him in passing at the clinic. He seemed glum."

"With any luck, we're driving him as crazy as he was driving us."

"You know what, Mona? I'm not really into this caper anymore. But please feel free to have a thing with Ben if you want to."

Mona said nothing for a long time, slowly stirring her whiskey sour with her swizzle stick.

Finally she looked up at Jessie with an annoyed expression. "Thanks, but I don't need your permission. You're not my mother."

Jessie gave a startled laugh. "I never imagined that I was!"

Jessie reflected that it probably made sense to keep your distance from other people. Who knew what insane archetypes existing only in their own addled brains they might try to wedge you into?

She looked out the window at the glimmering lights of Port Said, where terrorists disguised as crew had hijacked the *Achille Lauro* and murdered a man for being handicapped and Jewish. She and Mona sat in awkward silence as the ship moved into the Mediterranean. A brisk wind from the north began to clear out the torrid desert air, while a white-capped breaker lifted the giant ship toward the flickering stars that had popped out overhead.

During the night, the ship would dock at Alexandria. Charles Savage's corpse would be off-loaded there in the morning. Jessie would spend the day trying to decipher the city's appeal for Kat. How Mona spent her day was of no concern whatsoever to Jessie. Mona Paradiso, indeed! It sounded like a pseudonym for a porn star. No wonder the Met hadn't wanted her.

Chapter 10

Palimpsest

THEY WAITED UNTIL THE OTHER PASSENGERS HAD DEPARTED on their excursions around Alexandria before removing the body bag containing Charles Savage from the refrigerated morgue. Eva Cummings from Guest Services was standing on the quay with Gail Savage, who was wearing her now-signature dark glasses and black head scarf. Ben, in his whites, was talking to an Alexandrian harbor official. Pushing the gurney off the ship was the maintenance man who had fought the pirates so bravely. He kept glancing at Gail as though trying to catch her eye, but she refused to look at him. His face was haggard. He appeared to have it bad.

Jessie walked over to Gail. Gail removed her sunglasses, revealing her startling turquoise eyes. She said in a choked voice, "Thank you again, Doctor, for trying to save Charles that night."

"You're welcome," said Jessie. "I'm sorry I wasn't successful."

"I knew he had a bad heart, but I didn't realize how bad. I should have taken better care of him."

"Heart attacks are impossible to predict, Mrs. Savage. You shouldn't fault yourself." Gail seemed to have undergone a metamorphosis, from a narcissistic beauty queen to a perpetually grieving mourner on leave from Giotto's *Lamentation of Christ*.

"Thank you. That helps me with my guilt for not having been there when he needed me. It's hard to bear thinking about the wonderful life he gave me, and how I just took his kindness and generosity for granted."

Jessie blinked. Who was this woman? "Where is home?" she finally asked.

"Daytona Beach."

"So you're heading back there today?"

"No, I've decided to continue on the *Amphitrite* to Key West. I know Charles would want me to. He was so happy to be back at sea with his shipmates from the Battle of Okinawa. I'm going to buy an urn for his ashes so that he, too, can complete what was supposed to be our journey of a lifetime."

Jessie nodded, doing her best to convey the impression that she found this behavior sane. But it would never have occurred to her to bring Kat's ashes along, no matter how much Kat might have enjoyed this voyage while alive. Still, the cruise staff was required to endorse whatever guests said or did, so long as it wasn't illegal.

A battered black hearse pulled up, and the driver, a modern-day Charon in a black gabardine uniform worn shiny from over-use, helped the maintenance man load the body bag into the back. Gail got into the rear seat with Eva Cummings. Charon handed Ben some papers, shook his hand, and slid into the front seat. The antique hearse shuddered away to the city morgue for an autopsy, and then onward to the crematorium.

Jessie sauntered over to Ben. "Did you know that Mrs. Savage is finishing the cruise with her husband's ashes in an urn?"

Ben nodded. "What can I say? Both fares have been paid."

"May I have a few hours off today? There are some sites I want to visit."

"I see you've signed up to escort the bus tour to El Alamein tomorrow, so you should take the whole day off."

"Thanks, you're a pal," said Jessie.

Ben smiled his most fetching smile, the one that displayed his cavernous dimples. "Just a pal, huh?"

"So it would seem." She returned his fake smile.

"I think we must have grown too serious for casual sex, and too jaded for serious sex."

"Sounds about right. I think it's called maturity."

"I should probably have listened to you when you said that you just aren't that into men."

"What?" So now it was all about her, rather than about his wish to be with Mona instead? His duplicity had nothing to do with her lack of enthusiasm for his renewed pursuit of her?

"Never mind, Jessie, it's all good." He was employing youthful jargon now, no doubt seeing himself as Mona's peer, even though she was the age of some of his daughters. He strode jauntily back toward the vast ship, which towered a dozen stories above the quay, its many glass windows and doors reflecting the morning sun.

Jessie shrugged. Fortunately, she didn't really care what Ben thought or did.

XANDER STOOD ON THE QUAY BESIDE THE EMPTY GURNEY, watching the woman he loved ride away in a hearse with the chilled corpse of her husband. Gail had been avoiding him ever since her husband's death. He understood that she had to feign grief for her husband. But he was sure she would return to him once the required period of mourning was over. She was the most amazing woman he had ever made love to. There was nothing she wouldn't try. Pleasing women passengers was the way he had found to supplement his meager wages. Every crew member had his or her hustle. Some cut hair for other crewmates or gave massages. Others rented out porn or cleaned the cabins of those who could afford to pay. But Xander's chosen gig was to keep women passengers happy. In the beginning, Gail had been just another mark, strutting into the crew bar in her skinny jeans in search of some easy action with the help. But before he knew it, he'd fallen in love with her. She loved him, too, or at least that was what she moaned as he thrust into her time after time on the roof of the elevator to the cocktail lounge.

He had even begun to imagine a future with her. She was his ticket off this floating dungeon. It had to happen soon, though, before his back gave out again. He had ruptured a disk lugging baggage. The cruise company had paid for an operation and had covered his salary for several months. But he had been required to return to work while still in pain, and the exertions Gail had inspired in him hadn't helped his recovery. If he needed more time off or another operation, the cruise line would just cut him loose with no medical insurance and no income. The streets of Manila were lined with disabled cruise ship workers looking for physically undemanding land jobs.

When Gail's husband died, it seemed God's will. Now she would have his money and would be free to be Xander's wife. The only obstacle was his wife and three children back in the Philippines. He hadn't mentioned them to Gail yet. It would have ruined her image of him as a freebooting buccaneer. The knowledge that he was actually a dad and a husband might turn her off. But somehow he would find a way for Gail and himself to spend the rest of their lives together, smoking hash in the sun at her beachfront condo in Daytona Beach.

————

AT THE END OF THE QUAY LURKED SOME TAXIS WITH BLACK
roofs and fenders, and yellow chassis. Jessie took one along the
narrow isthmus that separated the cruise ship harbor from the
main bay, where hundreds of pleasure craft and fishing trawl-
ers with turquoise or golden trim and hulls were straining at
their mooring chains. Curving around the bay was the Corniche,
a sweeping crescent lined with eight- and ten-story apartment
blocks and hotels in a variety of Belle Epoque styles, some quite
dilapidated.

Partway around the Corniche, the minarets and cream-colored
domes of a mosque interrupted the skyline with a reminder of
who now ruled Egypt. On the far side of the crescent, a gigan-
tic disk that housed the new library reflected the morning sun.
The old library had allegedly been burned down by mistake by
Julius Caesar in 48 B.C. and had just now been replaced. Beyond
the library, on a tentacle of land extending into the sea, sat the
rococo summer palace of King Farouk, who, according to Kat's
notes, devoured six hundred oysters per week. He had fled that
palace for Italy on his royal yacht, anchored in this bay, following
Nasser's nationalist coup in the 1950s. Kat quoted him as having announced, "Soon there will be only five kings left—the King
of England, the King of Spades, the King of Clubs, the King of
Hearts, and the King of Diamonds."

The taxi arrived at a stunning fifteenth-century fortress of pale
stone with round crenellated towers, built by a sultan to fend off
Ottoman attacks. Jessie wandered around it, peering out at the
Mediterranean through slits cut for archers and larger openings
left for cannon barrels. The sea was being whipped into a froth by
a strong north wind. Waves were crashing on the seawalls below,

and large plumes of spray were leaping skyward, wavering and glittering in the sunlight.

No other tourists were present, since everyone was now afraid to visit Egypt. The many bored guards paid her no attention when she sat down on a parapet on the roof of the defensive tower. She removed Kat's notebook from her bag and read that Greeks had built the city in the third century B.C. Their 450-foot lighthouse had been a marvel of the ancient world. At night its furnace produced flames that could be seen thirty miles out to sea, to guide approaching ships into this harbor. It had been destroyed by earthquakes.

After the Roman navy defeated Cleopatra, Alexandria became a Roman colony. Her palace, where she had seduced Julius Caesar and Mark Antony, had borne four children by them, and had committed suicide after the Roman invasion, had also been destroyed by earthquakes and tsunamis. It now lay alongside sections of the toppled lighthouse under the water in the harbor where the fishing boats were bobbing.

Jessie returned the notebook to her bag and walked back across the causeway, past the gold and turquoise boats. Reaching the Corniche, she followed a sidewalk along the seawall. The beach below was cluttered with plastic grocery bags and drink bottles. The water itself was the unpleasant green of vomited bile. But some sunbathers were sitting at white plastic tables under garish beach umbrellas, watching their children frolic in the toxic water.

A multilane highway separated the bay from the buildings. The creeping cars beeped at one another constantly, like a flock of migrating geese. Clouds of exhaust fumes enveloped her as she strolled along the sidewalk, trying to figure out why Alexandria had so intrigued Kat as she lay dying. She looked around for a stoplight or crosswalk but could see none. She watched the other pedestrians. They just waited for an opening among the cars and then launched themselves into the traffic, hoping for the best. She copied them and lived to reach the other side.

Turning inland, Jessie wandered through a warren of narrow side streets, guided by a Google map on her iPhone. Eventually, she came to the dingy mustard apartment building where Cavafy had lived. The top half of its double wooden doors was decorated with wrought-iron arabesques. On the wall beside the entry, a polished brass plaque read CAVAFY MUSEUM in Greek. But a notice on the door said the museum was closed until further notice.

Jessie followed her Google map another mile to the Greek Orthodox cemetery. Passing through a gate and beneath a leafy arbor, she wandered around until she found Cavafy's gravestone, a white marble slab with a cross in relief toward its top. A waist-high iron fence in an Art Deco pattern threw a geometric shadow across the white marble, where someone had placed a rose that had withered. Tarnished Greek letters of inlaid copper spelled out his name and death date.

Jessie sat down among the palms and acacias on a bench with peeling green paint. She pulled out Kat's notebook and read that Cavafy, as he lay dying from throat cancer, unable to speak, had drawn on a piece of paper a period with a circle around it—a typesetter's mark, well known to every writer, meaning "full stop."

Next Kat wrote: "The Egyptians absorbed one invasion after another—Greek, Roman, Byzantine, Arab, French, British. Their outfits and monuments changed with each occupying army, yet they themselves remained Egyptian. They are currently disguised as Muslims. But their psyches have been shaped by the pharaohs and their pyramids. Layer upon layer of competing civilizations, yet the underlying essentials remain the same. The only constant in life is change."

Jessie reflected that she hadn't really seen Alexandria today. She had been too busy trying to see inside Kat's brain during those days when she had lain dying on the far side of the globe in a land of evergreens and snow. But the bread crumbs that Kat had scattered around Alexandria had led only to this deserted graveyard. Jessie had to confess that she was increasingly mystified by this woman with whom she had lived so happily for two decades. But had she really known her?

JESSIE ATE DINNER BY HERSELF AT A CORNER TABLE IN THE officers' lounge. In another corner huddled Mona and Ben, whispering back and forth and pointedly avoiding looking her way. She was annoyed. She had done nothing to merit becoming their scapegoat—a controlling mother for Mona and a man-hating dyke for Ben. That was the problem with living on a ship. Back home, she'd have just avoided them for several months. But if they needed her as an excuse to turn to each other for sexual solace, there was nothing she could do about it. So she returned to her cabin and continued her puzzled perusal of Kat's final journal.

To truly understand Cavafy, and therefore Kat's interest in him, Jessie realized she would need to go to Alexandria's red-light district late at night—if it still existed under Islamic rule. According to Kat, Cavafy had kept a room in a brothel there, in which he had entertained a parade of handsome young men who worked as dishwashers and hustlers. Kat had copied one of his poems that memorialized them:

Body, remember not just how much you were loved,
not just the beds where you have lain,
but also those longings that so openly
glistened for you in the eyes,
And trembled in the voice. . . .

Below this were several drafts of a poem Kat had evidently composed in response, with many crossed out words and arrows that shifted phrases here and there. The final version was titled "Swan Song I":

You've come undone, dear one.
Your shoulders show their scars.
So zip yourself up and march out my door—
Grit your teeth, clench your fists, hide your flinch.

Or else shrug those silk straps off your arms,
And stretch out beside me right now.
Let me tend to your wounds, soothe them with salve,
Bathe them, and bind them in balm.

I'll touch you so softly tonight, my love,
That you'll scarcely recall all that gall.
You'll cry as before, but this time for joy,
In the red through my window at dawn.

I know your chagrin. It's my own.
Hope guttered and gone out.
Promises scorched, trust turned to dust,
Ashes and soot, smoke on the wind.

But bloodroot can sprout in charred forests,
When swallows swoop home from the south.
As sun thaws the frost, mauve buds swell and burst—
Until snow spreads its shroud in the fall.

So stay with me now.
Hand me your pain.
Look in my eyes.
Let love live again.

Jessie laid down the journal. Kat had had her share of lovers before they met, just like every other child of the 1970s. She used to say that if gay marriage had been legal when she was in her prime, she'd have had as many ex-spouses as Zsa Zsa Gabor. But Jessie had always assumed that neither of them had been with other people while they were together. Was it possible Kat had had an affair during their relationship? Or did this poem refer to someone Kat had loved before they met? Or had it all existed only in Kat's imagination—a preliminary sketch of some character and situation she was inventing for her next novel? Was her interest in Cavafy because he had lived the life of some gay men, with casual sexual encounters whenever he pleased? Had Kat been secretly longing for a more adventurous love life than the one she had shared with Jessie?

Jessie struggled to get a grip. Kat had often traveled alone, doing lecture and reading tours. She had locked herself up for weeks at a time in big cities and isolated cabins to write her books uninterrupted. She had explained to Jessie that she had been the eldest daughter in a large family and had been required by her mother to baby-sit the younger children. To be alone was to her the ultimate luxury. But what if she hadn't really been alone?

Yet surely if Kat had been longing for or pursuing Cavafy's erotic lifestyle, she wouldn't have written about it in a journal that Jessie was bound to read. She wouldn't have wanted to hurt Jessie with such a startling revelation. But what if she'd been so out of it on morphine during her final days that she had simply forgotten to destroy this journal?

If Kat had been in love with someone else, why couldn't she have just said so? They would have dealt with it—or not. Jessie recalled an argument between them in their condo living room in which she had ended up asking Kat, "But why do you have to be so vague all the time? Why can't you just say what you mean?"

"Because I can't," Kat had replied. "I write novels to find out what I think and feel. You're lucky, because you seem to understand right away things that take me three hundred pages to figure out. But we southerners aren't noted for our intelligence."

"Don't pretend to me that you've just fallen off the turnip truck! You're the one who's published a dozen books."

"Creativity isn't the same thing as intelligence," Kat had replied.

THE NEXT MORNING, JESSIE NODDED TO RODNEY MULLINS and his wife as they climbed onto the tour bus. They sat down in the front seat opposite Jessie. Rodney was still limping from his fall off the top deck. As a veteran of the British army, though, he was apparently determined not to miss this daylong tour of El Alamein, to honor the World War II sacrifices of his brothers in battle.

Most cruise guests on the bus were veterans of some war or another, or wives of these veterans. They were the reason why the

Amphitrite had docked in Alexandria, despite its having bypassed the other Egyptian ports for being too dangerous. Many had signed on for this cruise precisely because of the stop at El Alamein. To have skipped it would have risked a riot by men who knew how to kill.

Gail Savage, attired in a black silk jumpsuit, with her black scarf corralling her mane of blond hair, boarded the bus. Behind her came a gentleman host named Harry, carrying a black leather Balenciaga tote bag containing a mahogany urn full of Charles's ashes. And behind Harry stretched a line of Charles's battleship comrades in their royal blue naval veteran caps, accompanied by their long-suffering wives, who sported Hermès scarves from the onboard boutique, tied in intriguing knots learned in the workshops conducted by Captain Kilgore's new bride.

Jessie had volunteered to be the ship representative on this trip. Several junior chefs were hosting a barbecue on a beach west of Alexandria. All staff and crew not on duty were invited, and many needed such a relaxing afternoon onshore after the stress of transiting the pirate playground and the Suez Canal with two thousand overwrought passengers. But Jessie felt that since she was the most recent addition to the staff, it was appropriate that she assume this bus duty so that others could go to the barbecue. In addition, both Mona and Ben had continued to change directions or duck through doorways when they saw her coming. She didn't relish an afternoon of watching them parade around in skimpy bathing suits, Ben prancing like a stallion pursuing a mare in heat.

Amira, the local tour guide, was sitting beside Jessie. She wore what Jessie was coming to recognize as a uniform for young Egyptian women—jeans, a tight T-shirt with long sleeves that covered her wrists, a loose colorfully patterned blouse, and a red head scarf that coordinated with the blouse. She was chatting through a microphone to the passengers in excellent British-accented English, describing the sites they were passing and summarizing the complicated history of Alexandria—from a seaside village of fishermen who worshipped Isis and Osiris, to a Greek city-state founded by Alexander the Great, to a colony of Rome, to a center for Sufi teachings following the expulsion of Muslims from Spain in the fifteenth century, to a watering hole for French and British expatriates. They were passing mile after mile of modern holiday complexes along the coast, as empty as ghost towns. Amira explained that they were occupied for only a couple of months in the summer, when people from Cairo headed north for the cool coastal breezes off the Mediterranean.

Jessie lacked the stamina to listen to Amira. Still shaken by "Swan Song I," she was trying to convince herself that it was fine if other people had looked at Kat with longing. After all, a few had looked at Jessie with longing, too—and a couple of times she had looked back. And what difference did it make now if either had done more than look?

Kat had had an imperious streak that resisted any attempt to control her. She said it was a result of having grown up a Southern Baptist, surrounded by so many prohibitions that you became determined to thwart them all. She embodied what people meant when they spoke of southern women's having iron fists inside their velvet gloves. Kat was implacably charming and polite, unless you tried to boss her around. Then she went all John Wayne on you, and her beautiful amber eyes turned to ice.

JESSIE STOOD TO ONE SIDE OF THE DOOR AS THE CRUISE guests climbed down from the bus. She watched Rodney Mullins limp alongside his handbag-clutching wife toward the group assembling around Amira. Gail Savage appeared in the bus doorway, with Harry behind her, toting the leather bag containing her husband's urn. Jessie held out a hand to help her down. Behind Harry filed Charles's honor guard of fellow sailors and their wives. They all wore headsets beneath their naval veteran caps that would allow them to hear Amira's commentary as she conducted them around the various sites.

A rectangular block of stone welcomed them to the cemetery. On it was carved, THEIR NAME LIVETH FOREVERMORE. And beyond it nearly eight thousand white marble headstones stretched out woefully among some spindly olive trees. As they trudged through the sandy soil, inspecting the identical graves, Jessie could hear Charles Savage's shipmates muttering to one another that 12,000 American soldiers and 100,000 Japanese had died on Okinawa, so why was El Alamein considered such a big deal?

Amira led them toward the museum. Outside it, they circled a garden where half a dozen varieties of tanks painted the color of sand were on display. A damaged Spitfire with twisted propeller blades perched on a concrete platform like a swatted mosquito. The garden resembled an adventure playground for delinquent teenagers. The men inspected the equipment, fascinated, while their wives discussed the new shades of nail polish available at the Canyon Ranch spa on the *Amphitrite,* where they all profoundly wished they were passing the day.

Inside, display cases featured mannequins in uniforms, wearing medals and carrying equipment and banners, organized by nation. A large sand table illustrated the two battles of El Alamein, using rows of blinking lights to indicate troop movements. Amira steered the group from display to display, explaining Rommel's and Montgomery's strategies. Between the two armies, more than 300,000 young men had wandered around a sandy wasteland, wearing only shorts and light sweaters in a place where hoarfrost formed on the jeep hoods at night. Many soldiers on both sides dropped dead from dehydration, hypothermia, and disease, to say nothing of bullets and mortars. Many deserters from both armies got lost trying to flee and simply lay down in the sand to perish. Many tanks and jeeps ran out of fuel and sat buried in sand drifts. Many mines remained unexploded and were still today blowing legs off of unlucky camels.

When they reached a display case covering a facet of the campaign labeled OPERATION MANHOOD, Jessie couldn't take it anymore. She excused herself to Amira and returned to the bus, where she rested her head against the seat back and felt despair. Whenever the physicians in her family were confronted with hopeless human lunacy, they muttered, "Poor suffering human-ity." Jessie, her son Anthony, and her brothers now did this, as had their father, as had his father and mother before him. It was their family mantra.

What struck Jessie most forcefully about this battlefield was the cleanliness and orderliness, the neat rows of graves so pre-cisely spaced. She was suddenly assailed by memories of her father as he lay in a bed in a nursing home north of Burlington during his final months.

Day after day, hour after hour, he spoke about war, "his" war, World War II. He had lived in a tent in the snow in northern France with one helmet of coal per day for heat. After contracting pneumonia, he had been sent to the American Hospital near Paris, where he spent every night lying under his bed while German planes roared past overhead. Back at his base, he had climbed down a ladder every morning into a huge pit dug in the ground in order to treat the German prisoners corralled there.

He had met trainloads of wounded and dying Allied soldiers shipped south from the Battle of the Bulge. Later, under a tarp in the Roman ruins of Trier, with a machine gun at his feet, he had operated on starving and diseased POWs liberated from German camps. One evening as he was saving the leg of a German prisoner from amputation, a group of retreating German soldiers broke into the operating tent and sprayed the doctors with bullets. Once they realized that the patient was German, they apologized, thanked the doctors for their humanity, and departed. Her father finished the procedure with bullets in his own legs, as well as a shattered kneecap.

"You were a hero, Dad," Jessie insisted.

"There was nothing heroic about it," he maintained with dogged urgency. "We were terrified the whole time. We just wanted to survive, and help each other survive, and get the hell back home. When I die, I don't want a military funeral. Flags and uniforms and twenty-one-gun salutes—no! It was all blood and feces and mud, rotting corpses and handsome young men with missing limbs, screaming with pain and fear. Confusion and horror and panic. No honor guard for me, Jessie. No taps on a lone bugle from a distant hillside. No folded American flag. No nothing. Please promise me." She promised him.

Later that week as Jessie was watching Saving Private Ryan *with him on TV, he got a terrified look on his face and shouted at her to go find flak jackets and helmets for them both. She tried to reassure him that they were safe in a nursing home in Burlington, but he was convinced they were under attack on Omaha Beach. A few nights later, she was summoned to his bedside in the middle of the night because he had awakened yelling and had hurled the night nurse across the room. He was transferred the next day to the locked ward for dementia patients.*

Back at his deserted house, as Jessie cleaned out his closets, she found his beige wool captain's dress uniform, with many medals and ribbons pinned on its chest. It was as pocked with moth holes as a battlefield with shell craters. He hadn't put it in a bag to protect it. It appeared he hadn't even looked at it for seventy years. Yet his wartime experiences had remained vivid and seemed to be increasing in intensity as he approached death.

Standing there in his closet with his moth-ravaged uniform clasped in her arms, Jessie suddenly understood that he had suffered from undiagnosed PTSD for seven decades. He had tried all that time to self-medicate with prescription painkillers, driving the local pharmacists crazy with his schemes to augment his stash. The whole family were physicians, and the symptoms had been right there in front of them. But even her brother Stephen, who had himself been treated for PTSD after his tour in Vietnam, hadn't recognized their father's dire condition. They were all so accustomed to his being in charge and taking care of everyone else that it hadn't occurred to them that he could ever need help. Jessie had been swamped with grief for him—and for his family, who had had to endure his never-ending anxieties and his fruitless attempts to alleviate them with ever-increasing doses of Dilaudid.

Soon after this, her father at last found release from his suffering: The hospice nurses gave him as much morphine as he wanted. He died peacefully, with Jessie and Stephen at his bedside, while Mozart's clarinet quintet played quietly on Stephen's iPhone.

The passengers were returning to the bus. Gail Savage got on first, Harry behind her with the tote bag. They sat down in the front seat opposite Jessie, where Rodney Mullins and his wife had been sitting on the trip over. While Jessie was trying to figure out how to inform them that they had just stolen Rodney's seat, Rodney climbed on the bus. He stood in the aisle and looked down at them, the flexing muscles in his beefy forearms making his snake tattoo writhe as though the snake were alive. "Excuse me, madam," he said icily, "but I think you've taken our seats."

Gail sighed plaintively and looked up at him through her enormous sunglasses. She removed them, no doubt intending to enchant him with her startling turquoise eyes. "My husband Charles's ashes are in this bag, and it's so heavy. We've been lugging it around all afternoon, and we're absolutely exhausted. Do you mind if we just stay here?"

Rodney looked at her with outrage. But he whirled around and limped down the aisle to Gail's seat in the back, with his wife trotting along behind him, clutching her handbag to her chest as protectively as though it contained the nuclear codes.

A TENT HAD BEEN SET UP ON THE QUAY ALONGSIDE THE *Amphitrite.* Waiters were serving the guests home from their tours flutes of Veuve Clicquot. As Jessie descended the bus steps, she spotted the young maintenance man in the red bandanna headband carrying a crate of bottles from the ship to the tent. A gangly ginger-haired man in a green polo shirt stood beside the tent, looking expectantly at the bus. Jessie realized it was Rusty Kincaid, the golf pro who had left the ship in Dubai with a wilted erection.

As she held out her hand to help Gail down the steps, the young man's face broke into a grin. When Gail spotted him, she stumbled and would have fallen if Jessie hadn't grabbed her arm to steady her. Behind her came Harry with the Balenciaga bag.

Rusty dashed over to Gail and seized her arm from Jessie.

"Where in the world did you come from?" Gail asked irritably.

"The airport! I'm getting back on the ship! I'm as good as new and ready to ride!" He gestured to her scarf and mourning gear. "But what's happened?"

"My husband, Charles, had a heart attack and died."

Rusty struggled to assume a somber expression. "No kidding," he finally said.

"Harry has been kind enough to carry his ashes for me today. We just took Charles to El Alamein."

Rusty glanced uneasily at Harry. Harry glared back. There was a crashing sound over by the drinks tent. Everyone looked up and saw that a maintenance man in a blue jumpsuit had dropped a crate of champagne bottles. A gasp went up from the crowd, many evidently knowing the price of a bottle of Veuve Clicquot.

Gail glanced in the direction of the crash. Her eyes met those of the maintenance man. She flushed while he blanched, as though they were exchanging blood supplies. People stalled behind Gail on the bus started to mutter, eager to get to the champagne before it ran out.

"Will you dine with me tonight?" Rusty asked Gail as the passengers fought their way past her to the waiters whose trays bore the champagne flutes.

"That's hardly appropriate now that I'm a widow," she sniffed.

Jessie reflected that this sudden seizure of propriety didn't really suit her.

"Can I come to your room after dinner, then?" He wriggled his rust-colored eyebrows so that they looked like the woolly bear caterpillars that old-time Vermonters inspected to predict the severity of the upcoming winter.

"I've been out all day. I'm going to order room service and go right to sleep."

"Tomorrow, then?" asked Rusty, his bubbly good spirits starting to go flat.

"We'll see," she murmured, heading for the ship.

After the final passenger had exited from the bus, Jessie walked over to the tent and took a champagne flute from a waiter. The maintenance man who had dropped the Veuve Clicquot was carrying out another case. He set it on a table and straightened up, his hands bracing his lower back, a pained expression on his face.

"Spine troubles?" ventured Jessie.

He nodded. "I had a disk operation, but I haven't felt that great ever since."

"You shouldn't be carrying crates of champagne, for one thing."

He shrugged. "What choice do I have?"

Jessie nodded. "Sorry, it's your job, isn't it? I'm Jessie, by the way." She extended her hand.

He reached out his grimy hand and they shook. "Xander," he said. "Nice to meet you, Doctor."

"I admired your throwing those tables at the pirates in the Red Sea."

"You have to fight fire with fire, right?"

"Unless you're the brand of Christian who believes you should turn the other cheek. But picking up tables is another thing you shouldn't do, Xander, for the sake of your poor back."

Xander cast her a winning smile. "Thank you, Doctor. I'll make sure not to throw tables at pirates in the future!"

Jessie smiled back. He was cheeky and good-looking, in a stevedore kind of way. It was clear something was going on between him and Gail Savage. She could see why Gail was attracted to him. But why were women so often drawn to bad boys? Probably they got so sick of being good girls that bad boys represented an escape. Of course many men and some lesbians preferred bad girls, as well. Jessie herself would have dated Mary Magdalene over the Virgin Mary any day.

Chapter 11

The Love Cave

JESSIE LEFT HER CABIN AND HEADED FOR THE TOP DECK. As she passed Gail Savage's new suite, Harry, the gentleman host, darted from the hallway into the closet where the cleaners stored their supplies. Jessie stood still, waiting for him to realize that he'd walked into a closet and reappear. But he never did. So she continued down the carpeted corridor, spotting Xander at the far end, striding away in his blue jumpsuit, carrying a red toolbox.

When she turned the corner into the elevator landing, she almost ran into Rusty Kincaid. He blushed to the roots of his curly ginger hair.

"How's it going, Rusty?"

"Fine, Doctor. I'm as good as new!"

"Glad to hear it. But I'm afraid I can't linger. I'm on my way to watch a meteor shower. I'll see you later."

"I hope not!"

They both laughed.

As the elevator ascended, Jessie reflected that during the days since departing from Alexandria all three of these men had been in hot pursuit of Gail. When she was in her suite, they kept watch at her doorway, like the Pope's Swiss Guard, casting evil glances at one another. And when she emerged, they circled her like sweat bees, vying with one another to carry the Balenciaga tote containing the cremation urn. Gail appeared deeply uninterested in all of them, but who knew what might be going on in her suite in the middle of the night? Something she was or wasn't doing seemed to be keeping all three men as bewitched as Snow White's dwarfs.

It had also become apparent to Jessie that Ben and Mona had consummated their flirtation. They huddled together, giggling, every chance they got, ramping up their displays of affection whenever Jessie appeared. But it was okay. She wasn't much interested in either of them anymore.

When Jessie reached the top deck, she grabbed a cushion off a lounge chair and lay down on it on her back. The breeze off the water was stiff, and the swells were running high. But the pollution-free night sky was clear, and the stars sparkled like a rapper's bling. Jessie recognized many of the constellations from Girl Scout camp on Lake Champlain. As she traced the familiar patterns and reviewed the associated legends composed eons ago by lonely shepherd boys in moonlit pastures, she felt her true insignificance. She was an amoeba poised on a tiny sphere that was afloat in this unimaginably vast sea of astral bodies. Nothing that she or anyone else said or did was of any significance whatsoever.

On clear summer nights, she and Kat used to drift around Lake Champlain on their pontoon boat, studying these same constellations. They had concluded that it was impossible that some of these trillions of stars didn't host planets inhabited by other sentient creatures. Kat had suggested that Earth was a boot camp for such a planet. They sent their youth to Earth to experience violence and evil, thereby learning the value of peace and compassion. Only then were the children allowed to return home. If they misbehaved, they were threatened with being sent back to Earth, like a toddler's time-out.

Kat had also speculated that these more evolved creatures were cultivating Earth, like some garbage-strewn, rat-infested junkyard. When dinosaurs became too repulsive, these superior beings directed an asteroid at Earth to destroy the giant reptiles, clearing the way for small mammals to emerge from the undergrowth and evolve into human beings. If humans didn't shape up soon, Kat maintained that another asteroid would arrive to prepare Earth for the implantation of a less clueless species.

Suddenly the steady thrum of the ship's engine accelerated, and the ship veered sharply to the right, causing Jessie to roll off her cushion. At the same time her beeper started pinging. She discovered a message from Ben, summoning her to the bridge. Shaking off her cosmic ruminations, she jumped up and ran for the door to the elevator.

Ben was already engrossed in an intense discussion with Captain Kilgore and several bridge officers when she arrived. Captain Kilgore was explaining that an inflatable rubber boat containing a dozen refugees had been spotted by a surveillance plane at dusk, drifting in high seas a few miles to starboard. They had frantically waved shirts and towels at the plane. The Italian coast guard was requesting that the *Amphitrite* take these people on board and provide food, water, and medical care. The cruise ship would then proceed to its planned stop at Gozo, in the Maltese Islands, where the coast guard would take charge of them the next day.

"We have no choice," announced Captain Kilgore. "It's our legal obligation under maritime law to aid any vessel in distress."

"Also our moral obligation," murmured Ben.

Jessie glanced at him, impressed.

Captain Kilgore issued instructions, and soon the "Man Overboard" siren was blaring. After it had finished, he switched on the PA system and explained to the guests what was happening.

Ben, Jessie, and Amy loaded the crash cart with supplies at the clinic and took it down to the bottom deck, where the other nurses were setting up cots in an empty storage room. After organizing their triage area, they walked to the open cargo door to see what was going on outside. Jessie spotted a couple of Zodiacs descending on cables along the flank of the ship. Spotlights suddenly illuminated the water off the starboard side. Nearby, the foundering boat was lurching back and forth in the swells, its panicked passengers clutching the side handles. The rubber pontoons looked soft, as though slowly deflating.

The Zodiacs motored close to the imploding vessel, and their crews began to hurl life vests and buoys into the boat. They called out to the passengers, trying to calm them and coax them into donning the life jackets. Meanwhile, the implacable swells kept lifting the capsizing boat high up into the air, like a carnival ride gone rogue.

Ben muttered to Jessie, "The water temperature must be about sixty degrees Fahrenheit. Let's hope they can get those people off that boat before it sinks, or we'll be dealing with hypothermia, along with everything else."

Jessie nodded. Whatever personal issues they might have were now isolated behind a firewall of professional efficiency. All that mattered was getting those unfortunate people aboard and dealing with their health issues.

The crew in one Zodiac managed to toss a line to a man in the boat. The Zodiac slowly towed the boat over to the *Amphitrite,* where men on the cargo deck helped the refugees board. One middle-aged man with coils of sodden gray hair was holding a young girl in his arms. He refused to let go of her as he climbed up to the deck and passed through the door into the ship.

Ben and Jessie ushered the shivering people into the storage room, where the nurses helped them out of their soaked clothes and wrapped them in silver foil space blankets. Then Ben and Jessie took their vital signs and assessed the status of their hearts and lungs with stethoscopes. It seemed they were South Sudanese. Jessie spoke no Arabic, so she worked in silence, trying to make her smiles reassuring.

The man with the young girl in his arms still wouldn't put her down. When Jessie walked over to him, she could smell the putrid odor of decomposition. The girl was dead. Her body was limp instead of rigid, so she must have died two or three days earlier. She looked to be about ten years old, the age of one of Jessie's granddaughters.

"Please, sir, I need to examine you," she said gently. "Can you give me your child?" She gestured to illustrate what she was saying.

The man shook his head. "You see, madam, she's my daughter," he said in British-inflected English. "We're going to Italy so she can attend school."

"You speak English?"

"I teach English at a Christian college in my country."

As Jessie continued to question him, she learned that a government militia had attacked his school. Several soldiers had raped his daughter. His wife had tried to stop them. They had raped her, as well. She fought so fiercely that they finally killed her. The soldiers promised that if the college didn't shut down, they would return. The surviving staff had pooled their money and traveled in a series of trucks and buses to a Libyan beach, where they were loaded onto this rubber boat. After several hours at sea, the engine conked out. The pilot placed a call on his satellite phone. A speedboat arrived to pick him up. When the teacher tried to prevent him from leaving, someone in the speedboat shot the teacher with a handgun.

The boat had drifted for a couple of days in the hot sun. Food and water ran out. People saved and drank their own urine. One man drank seawater and died. They hadn't wanted to abandon him, so they kept his body in the boat. The teacher's daughter developed a high fever and went into convulsions.

"Can you help her, Doctor? We have to get to Italy."

For once in her life, Jessie was speechless.

"I'll be right back," she finally said. She went over to Ben and explained the situation.

Ben approached the man and said, "Sir, we need to examine you. Would it be all right if my colleague here holds your daughter for you?"

The man hesitated, then said, "I suppose so."

He carefully handed the girl to Jessie. Jessie stood there with the limp little girl in her arms, noting how cold a body became once the life force had departed. At least her face appeared peaceful, in contrast to those of the refugees still alive.

The teacher seemed to be in pain, but Ben could locate no broken bones, no cuts, no blood. Then he discovered a hole the size of his baby fingertip in the man's right thigh, and a similar hole through the muscle of his upper right arm, and a third in his right calf. Ben and Jessie agreed that the holes were bullet wounds, puckered by the salt water. They also agreed that since no vital organs or blood vessels appeared to have been impacted, the bullets were best left in place.

As Ben bandaged the wounds, he persuaded the man to let Jessie carry his daughter's body into the next room, where the corpse of the man who had drunk the seawater was lying on a bed of ice bags. After agreeing, the father doubled over and began to weep. Ben stroked his back, looking as though he, too, might start crying.

Crew from the ship laundry began to gather the piles of wet clothing into their carts. Some kitchen staff served the survivors water, hot tea, and broth, cautioning them with hand signs to rehydrate slowly.

As Jessie and Ben walked back toward the clinic with their equipment, Jessie heard Captain Kilgore on the PA overhead, addressing the entire ship:

"Our staff and crew have just saved the lives of nearly a dozen of our fellow human beings, so we should all sleep well tonight, feeling proud that we rose to this occasion. Our new guests will be transferred to the Italian coast guard tomorrow morning for transport to a welcome center on Sicily, where their status will be assessed."

"What will happen to that girl's body?" Jessie asked Ben.

"I guess she'll be off-loaded on Malta. When this exodus from Africa began, the local people buried drowned migrants with prayers and flowers. But there have been so many since then that I think they're overwhelmed."

"What will happen to the rest of these people?"

"As I understand it, any political refugees whose lives are in danger will be allowed to stay in Europe. Those just wanting a better life will probably be returned to South Sudan."

"I'd say the lives of all these people are in danger, from what I've heard about those militias."

"I know," said Ben. "I wouldn't want to be the one making those decisions."

————

BACK IN HER CABIN, JESSIE STEPPED OUT OF HER DAMP scrubs and stuffed them into her laundry bag. Then she stood in a hot shower until her arms, which had held the young girl's violated body for such a long time, stopped trembling. She dried herself and pulled on some sweatpants and a T-shirt.

She switched on her computer to the Haydn quartet Mona had recommended. Lying down on her bed, she breathed deeply and allowed the stately music to soothe her. But as she struggled to put out of her head the image of that little girl being gang-raped, she began to cry. A tsunami of grief swept over her, and she sobbed, gasping for breath. How could she continue to live in a world like this?

She heard a tentative knock at her door. Thinking it might be Ben needing to discuss a patient, she wiped her face with her sheet and got up, clearing her throat and blowing her nose into a tissue. She fluffed up her still-damp hair with her fingertips.

Mona was standing there in a black satin robe decorated with scarlet Art Nouveau lilies. "I heard you crying through the wall. Is there anything I can do?"

Jessie hesitated. Then she stepped aside. "Come in." She gestured to the bed, the only place to sit in the small cabin.

Mona sat down, swung her legs up onto the mattress, and leaned back against the pillows. Jessie plopped down across from her in the desk chair, noting with relief that the Haydn quartet had ended. She didn't want Mona to think that she had paid any attention to her annoying come-on.

"Sorry to have disturbed you," said Jessie. "I forget how thin these walls are."

"Rough night?"

"You have no idea." Struggling not to, Jessie started crying again.

Mona scooted over toward the wall and patted the mattress.

"I thought you saw me as Cruella de Vil now," said Jessie.

"What happened tonight makes our little spats seem pretty ridiculous, doesn't it?"

Jessie stood up and walked over to the bed. Against her better judgment, she lay down beside Mona. Tentatively, they moved into each other's arms. Jessie laid her head on Mona's chest and began to sob again. Mona hesitantly patted her back and stroked her shoulders. Gradually, Jessie calmed down. She concentrated on timing her breathing to Mona's. Beneath her ear she could hear the steady thump of Mona's heart. Soon her own heart began to beat in tandem with Mona's. It had been a long time since she had found solace in the healing warmth of a woman's body. They just lay there, breathing in unison, hearts beating in sync, until both fell asleep.

THE SHIP HAD ALREADY DOCKED AT GOZO WHEN JESSIE woke up. She watched sunbeams reflected off the harbor water as they danced on the cabin ceiling. Her grief over the young girl's rape had transmuted overnight into anger, anger against all the bullies of this world. It was a familiar anger that she now realized had often percolated in her at the ER as she had repaired the results of their horrific brutalities. Her patients' physical wounds could often be healed, but their psychic wounds suppurated for a lifetime. It was beginning to look as though her famous detachment was only skin-deep.

"There. That wasn't so bad, was it?" Mona sat up beside her, smiling.

"It was kind of you to comfort me last night, Mona. I don't know when I've felt such despair."

Mona crawled to the end of the bed and stood up, tightening the belt on her satin robe. Her auburn hair was disheveled. She studied Jessie. "Would you like more than comfort from me, Jessie?"

After a long pause, Jessie replied, "I love you, Mona, but not like that."

Mona smiled faintly. "Okay. But just tap on my wall if you change your mind."

"I wouldn't want to disturb you and Ben."

Mona blushed. "Ben is just a diversion."

Jessie shrugged. Mona had behaved like a brat recently, and Jessie wasn't ready to forgive her. It was concession enough that she had acknowledged the love that was apparently stirring between them.

Realizing Jessie wasn't going to respond any further, Mona turned and left the cabin.

Jessie suddenly remembered that she had signed up to escort a bus trip to the cave where Calypso had imprisoned Odysseus as her love slave for seven years. She had read up on Homer on Wikipedia so she could answer guests' questions. Calypso had enchanted Odysseus with her singing. Odysseus was supposed to be going back home to Ithaca, but his love for Calypso held him captive there in her labyrinthine cavern. Finally, Zeus commanded Calypso to set Odysseus free so he could complete his mission. Calypso was deeply annoyed that gods got to have endless love affairs with mortals but objected when goddesses did the same. Clearly, sexism was nothing new.

Jessie turned on her TV to check the tour schedule. She discovered that the trip had been canceled because the love cave had collapsed during a recent earthquake.

Chapter 12

Slave to Love

THE MOOD ON THE *AMPHITRITE* WAS GLUM. MANY starboard-side passengers had watched from their balconies as the Sudanese refugees nearly sank into the sea. Several had come to the clinic in the days afterward requesting antidepressants. Those who were not complete sociopaths had realized that they had been born into Western democracies through no merit of their own. They had paid tens of thousands of dollars to ride this luxury liner, eating and drinking themselves into prediabetic stupors, while others rode capsizing ghost ships, drinking their own urine.

To cheer them up, Mitch, the cruise director, had announced a Texas barbecue on the roof deck that evening, during which the ship would transit the Strait of Gibraltar. Once into the Atlantic Ocean, there would be a special sunset surprise!

While the passengers worked on their cowboy outfits, Jessie remained in her cabin and continued her puzzled perusal of Kat's journal, still bewildered by "Swan Song I." Propped on her pillows, she read in Kat's handwriting: "Cavafy's fixation on beautiful young men isn't one I've ever shared. I've got two sons, so I know what pathetic creatures handsome young men really are."

Then came a clipping from a magazine review of Kat's third novel, which she had pasted into the journal, highlighting with a yellow marker: "Ms. Justice has allowed her feminist agenda to hijack her comedic gift. Please return to satire, Ms. Justice, and lose the soapbox."

Jessie recalled how annoyed Kat had been by this review. Her first novel had garnered lots of praise as a "madcap romp" set in commune days. Its more serious successors hadn't been as enthusiastically received. Beneath this quote Kat had written, "When men write about what they think and feel, it's called Truth. But when women do the same, it's called an agenda. I don't think I can write comedy anymore. This world no longer amuses me."

Then she had added, "How do you write honestly about gay experience without destroying your chance of being published and reviewed by mainstream presses? Is it possible? Cavafy didn't even try. Once he started writing candidly about his male lovers, he no longer published his poems. He just circulated typescripts to sympathetic friends.

"Vita Sackville-West tried to solve this dilemma by making a woman in each of her female couples male. But for this reason, some of her fiction doesn't ring true. By trying to make yourself acceptable to the conventional world, you falsify your own reality.

"Marguerite Yourcenar created protagonists who were gay males living in the distant past. Thus, readers could never claim that her novels were autobiographical—even though she lived for forty years with another woman. She was widely praised for writing like a man. If she had written like the lesbian that she was, whatever that entails, would she have been elected to the Académie française?

"Proust turned the men he yearned for into women in his fiction. E. M. Forster wrote *Maurice* in 1914, based partly on his love affair with a man in Alexandria. But it wasn't published until 1971, after his death. Who knows what amazing fiction gay writers might create if we weren't forced into straitjackets, so to speak, in order to earn a living or avoid ridicule? Self-censorship is the most insidious kind."

So did this lament explain Kat's interest in Cavafy? It wasn't that she admired his busy erotic life. It was, rather, that she was trying to figure out how to write about a gay person's perceptions without being penalized and pilloried for it. And she had apparently concluded, as had Cavafy, that it was impossible.

Jessie flipped back to "Swan Song I" and reread it. Then she closed the journal and leaned back on her pillows. Who was this mystery woman Kat had fantasized about? Or was it a real woman whom Kat had pursued in secret? Jessie had been so busy during Kat's final year, doing her job so she could pay their bills, and overseeing Kat's tests and treatments, that she probably hadn't taken the time to be very comforting to Kat about her approaching death. In any case, Kat had been such a stoic that she had appeared not to need it. Had someone else come along who was more comforting? One of the hired caregivers who came to the condo? A nurse at the hospital? Had the encounter in the poem really happened, or was Kat just wishing that it would? Surely she had been too sick to conduct or participate in a new seduction. But what a horrible way for Kat's and her romance to end—with her not knowing if Kat had been in love with someone else when she died.

Jessie realized that her imagination was running riot. She would have been able to tell if Kat had been involved with someone else. Besides, Kat wasn't devious. She would have told Jessie if this were so. In any case, Jessie had no choice but to exile this ridiculous suspicion from her mind. Otherwise, it might embitter her for the rest of her life. She grabbed her running shoes and laced them up. She would clear her mind with fresh air and mindless exertion.

As she exited through the heavy door onto the walking deck, she spotted Ben coming toward her in his officer whites, along with Mona in a mauve tracksuit. Jessie was irritated to feel a surge of pleasure at the sight of Mona. Dear God, when would it ever end, this ordeal of being drawn to another person like a sea turtle to a sandy beach on a full-moon night? She and Mona had had several brief encounters since passing the night in each other's arms—a coffee here, a chat there. Jessie found herself inventing excuses to detour past the theater on errands. A couple of times she had bumped into Mona near the clinic, where Mona had no business being. When Jessie tried to figure out what she had meant when she told Mona that she loved her, she realized that she was acknowledging a need they both seemed to feel simply to be together. It apparently soothed them both.

Mona looked embarrassed. Ben looked—what? He looked smug, an older man who had snared an attractive younger woman. So Mona probably hadn't told him about her night with Jessie. If she had, he would be looking licentious right now as he schemed about how to get them both into bed with him at once. Jessie waved at them and kept walking fast in the opposite direction.

DRESSED IN HER SKIRTED OFFICER'S UNIFORM, JESSIE walked out on the top deck. It was packed with oil tycoons in ten-gallon hats, Miss Kittys from *Gunsmoke,* a Lone Ranger in a black mask, several Davy Crocketts in fringed leather, renegade Indians and kerchiefed bandits, and some Dolly Partons. Many were swilling Jack Daniel's or Coronas. Ribs from an entire herd of steers were roasting on smoking grills tended by a platoon of chefs in tall white hats. Long tables held huge vats of coleslaw, baked beans, and potato salad. Platters were piled high with sliced tomatoes and ears of corn. Giant baking tins held oozing fruit cobblers. It felt obscene to Jessie after her night with the starving refugees, but she kept her gloomy thoughts to herself.

Mitch, the cruise director, wore sleeve garters and a brocade vest. It was unclear whom he thought he was impersonating. Bat Masterson maybe? He yelled through a microphone until he had quieted the crowd enough to announce that the line-dancing class was going to perform a new routine called "Cotton-Eyed Joe." Recorded country music blasted across the roof deck, and the dancers launched into a number that involved circling their arms overhead, as though lassoing steers, while shuffling their boots in intricate patterns. They wore cowboy hats, which they periodically removed to twirl in time to the music.

Rodney's twisted ankle must have healed, because he was schottishing with the best of them. And the best of them was unquestionably Mrs. Pendragon, the permanent passenger, who was giving quite a show in her tight jeans, pearl-snapped cowboy shirt, and tooled leather boots, hopping and stomping and slapping her boot heels. No one could have ever guessed that this good-time gal passed her days sewing miniature wedding gowns for aborted fetuses.

Once their dance had concluded, Captain Kilgore took Mitch's mike and said, "If you'll look off our starboard side, you can see the famous Rock of Gibraltar, one of the Pillars of Hercules. And off our port side is the other pillar, Morocco's Jebel Musa. On these pillars in ancient days was said to be posted the message *'Ne plus ultra,'* meaning 'No more beyond,' a warning to sailors not to venture into the dangerous ocean that raged on the far side of the pillars. And, in fact, you will need to hold tight to your drinks tonight, folks, because it can get rather rough in the strait. An upper current of water flows from the Atlantic into the Mediterranean, while a lower current flows in the opposite direction. Vikings used to sail their longships through this strait on the current alone, and German U-boats turned their engines off so they could drift into the Mediterranean undetected by Allied sentries on the shore. Enjoy your barbecue supper. I'll be back to reveal our special sunset surprise once we reach the Atlantic!"

Jessie moved to the starboard railing to inspect the Rock, which resembled a crouching lion. The sails of some windsurfers billowed at its base. Farther out, a couple of small fishing boats were trolling through the turbulent waters. In the distance straight ahead a ferry was crossing from Spain to Morocco.

Ben came over to her. Their night of dealing with the refugees had apparently convinced them both that it was unseemly to feud with each other when they were among the most fortunate people who had ever roamed the planet. Observing him that night, Jessie had recognized what a skilled physician he was—and also what a compassionate man, apart from his torturous affairs of the heart. He was an interesting man, as well, with his fascination with archaeology and paleoanthropology. There was a reason she had loved him all those years ago, and she had to confess that she still liked him very much. He was like a brother to her. They were similar in so many ways that it was no wonder their romance had fizzled. It had probably felt vaguely incestuous to them both.

"That rock is where the last Neanderthals died about forty thousand years ago," he was saying.

"Really? What happened to them?"

"Nobody knows for sure. They used to live all over what's now western Europe. They might have been slaughtered by the

Homo sapiens who arrived from Africa. Or *Homo sapiens* might have brought diseases Neanderthals had no immunities to. Or the warming weather might have weakened Neanderthals, since their bodies had been designed for an ice age. But before they died out, they must have had some wild nights with our distant ancestors, because everyone alive today contains some of their DNA. Except for Africans with no European or Asian ancestry."

Mitch was calling for everyone's attention, so they returned to the dance area. A song by Shania Twain called "Whose Bed Have Your Boots Been Under?" erupted from the speakers. Some dogs caged in the kennels down the deck began to howl. A dozen chefs suddenly deserted their grills to invade the dance floor like a flash mob. Waving their butcher knives and barbecue tongs, they performed the Electric Slide in unison in their sauce-stained aprons and tall white hats. One chef took center stage to juggle three butcher knives, while the audience whistled and cheered and twirled their white napkins over their heads.

Then Mitch invited the passengers to the buffet tables. People piled up their plates and headed to the chairs and dining tables and cushioned sea chests full of life jackets scattered all around the deck. Mrs. Pendragon and several of her dance team snagged Jessie to sit at their table as she passed by.

"I loved your new dance, Mrs. Pendragon," said Jessie.

"Please," said Mrs. Pendragon. "Just call me Mrs. P., the way everyone else does. But you should come to our class sometime."

"Thanks, maybe I will." Jessie mused that line dancing might be one way to avoid brooding in her cabin over Kat's infidelity that had probably never happened—and over the memory of that limp little body she had cradled in her arms.

Mona mounted the central dais, disguised as a Spanish flamenco dancer in a long red dress with flounces around the hem.

Drago had parted and slicked back her auburn hair to resemble a severe bun and had placed a huge fake scarlet hibiscus blossom at the nape of her neck. A man in a fedora accompanied her, carrying a guitar. He sat down and began playing an introduction that involved a lot of backhanded flicking of his fingers across the strings in a stabbing rhythm. Mona began to sing in Spanish. The song kept shifting from a major key to a minor one and back again. Jessie knew enough Spanish to follow the lyrics, which were expressing gratitude to life for all its gifts to human beings—the most precious one being love.

Mona gazed unabashedly at Jessie as she sang this. Her magnificent voice exuded an optimism much appreciated by the assembled guests, many of whom were still quite disturbed by the refugees' ordeal.

All of a sudden, Gail Savage moved out on the dance floor, wearing a long black dress with a skintight skirt that cupped her shapely buttocks. She was also wearing her usual black head scarf and sunglasses, as well as black stiletto heels with pointed toes and ankle straps. Harry was beside her, attired as a gaucho in a red kerchief, leather chaps, tight boots, and a black hat with a wide, flat brim.

With a flourish, Harry grabbed a butcher knife from one of the chefs. Gail reached down and seized the hem of her skirt. As she stretched it taut, Harry slashed her side seam all the way up to her hip. The audience gasped. It was like watching bad porn. Underneath the skirt Gail was wearing a black bodysuit and fishnet stockings. She was without a doubt the most erotic mourner Jessie had ever witnessed. The rumor around the ship was that Harry had been a priest. If this was true, he appeared to be making up for all the time he had lost being pious.

Gail moved into Harry's outstretched arms, and they began

to dance an agonizingly slow tango to Mona's song. As it progressed, Gail and Harry assumed some truly astonishing poses, with Gail stretched out supine while Harry held her just a foot off the floor, his mouth hovering inches above her ruby lips. Then he lifted her to her feet, and she flicked her heels backward at him several times, like a colt frolicking in spring sunshine, the sharp talons of her shoes barely missing his crotch. Men all over the deck reflexively folded their hands in front of their groins. Jessie watched with admiration as Gail wove her long fishnet-clad legs behind and between Harry's legs, and around his waist, without missing a beat, flashing enticing glimpses of her black bodysuit. She was like an octopus with rhythm.

Gail and Harry left the dance floor amid thunderous applause. As Gail passed the table at which Rodney Mullins and his wife sat, she bumped it with her hip. Rodney's drink skittered across the tabletop and fell into his lap. His face at first registered surprise, then discomfort as the chilly liquid soaked his crotch—and finally, fury. Gail's bumping his table had appeared deliberate, but who would mess with a man who had a serpent snaking up his forearm?

Rusty Kincaid was sitting at Gail and Harry's table, looking defeated. What could he possibly do with Gail to equal that libidinous display? Xander lay on his back beneath one of the grills, tinkering at it with a wrench and looking wretched. Jessie noticed that Charles's mahogany urn was also sitting in a chair at Gail's round table. On its top perched Charles's naval veteran cap.

As the applause faded, a woman disguised as Loretta Lynn, in a ruffled square-dancing skirt and cowboy boots, climbed up on the dais and grabbed the mike from Mona. "I want everyone here tonight to know that that woman you're all applauding stole my new gown from the laundry room before I'd worn it even once!"

she yelled in a broad Australian accent. "And she also burned my arm on purpose with a hot iron!"

The crowd fell silent and stared at Gail.

Gail sipped her Jack Daniel's, not even bothering to look at her accuser.

"Admit it, bitch!" screamed the woman. "You know it's true!"

Mitch rushed out, wrested the mike from the woman, handed it to Mona, and ushered the woman toward the elevator, talking to her soothingly.

As everyone watched, Gail gestured dismissively with her hand, as though flicking aside an annoying gnat.

Mona quickly said something to her guitar player. He began to strum, and she started singing "Slave to Love," with lyrics that described how loving a woman leads to obsession and ruin. Her eyes once again sought out Jessie as passengers got up and began to two-step, the men twirling the women in front of them while they circled the dance area. A blast of wind swept across the deck, carrying someone's Stetson over the railing, where it floated for a moment before tumbling toward the ocean. A flock of passing seagulls seemed to pause in mid-flight to discuss the identity of this strange new bird.

While Mrs. P. and her friends got up to join the two-steppers, Jessie remained seated, watching Mona in her stunning red dress, which displayed an even more stunning cleavage. She could feel Mona's attraction to her in the intensity of the gazes she kept directing at her. But what did Mona really want? Was she experiencing love, or was it just an attraction based on her need for some financial security as her voice underwent the challenges of aging? Did she want a patron, or a mother—or a lover? Mona was trying her best to make it work with Ben, but she had mentioned having had girlfriends. And once you had experienced the tenderness of a skilled woman, it was sometimes difficult to revert to the rough-and-tumble of a man.

Jessie wished she could give Mona what she appeared to want. She could certainly make love to her once or twice, but then it would be over—because Jessie was still haunted by Kat. But she could also see so clearly what would happen if it didn't end: She was in early old age, whereas Mona was just entering middle age. In a few years, Jessie would be seriously old. Mona would stay with her out of love and duty. But she would come to feel uninterested in Jessie's sagging flesh and would long for her freedom. Kat had been a few years older than Jessie, but they had grown up together before growing older together.

Mona might say tonight that "once or twice" would be just fine with her. But it wouldn't be fine with Jessie. Lovemaking was a fuel. Why rev the engines if you weren't going anywhere? Besides, she had had too much experience not to know that one-night stands between women were often disappointing. Good lovemaking for most required time. You had to learn what pleased the other person and explore new ways. You had to develop trust. In reality, most women weren't all that thrilled by the danger and novelty of the unknown.

Men were cursed with the biological imperative of spreading their seed as widely as possible. Danger and novelty turned them on. But women were left having to raise the seedlings. So women were cursed with the biological imperative of caution. It took an act of courage to allow foreign objects to enter your orifices. The stakes were high, and penalties for the losers, severe. Jessie had dealt with them all in her ER—pregnancy, HIV, HPV, herpes, syphilis, gonorrhea, chlamydia, fecal incontinence, battery, murder, suicide. To pretend these dangers weren't real, as many women did, was to betray your deepest instinct, one that went even deeper than desire—that of self-preservation. As you got older, you realized that wisdom often consisted of doing nothing.

Mitch took the mike from Mona and announced, "We've been fortunate to have had such calm conditions for our passage through the strait. We are now commencing the Atlantic portion of our voyage. We would like to invite you all to the bow to enjoy a concert by our wonderful *Amphitrite* orchestra, along with a complimentary glass of Veuve Clicquot. Our promised surprise is yet to be revealed!"

It took a long time for the wranglers on the roof deck to reach the bow and acquire their free champagne. Meanwhile, the orchestra played hits from *Les Misérables* and *The Phantom of the Opera,* while a few inexhaustible couples fox-trotted along the railings. The guests began to occupy the rows of folding chairs that looked out across the nose of the ship, where the sun was inching toward the horizon.

Once everyone was seated, the orchestra fell silent. Captain Kilgore appeared, the sinking crimson sun backlighting his crisp white dress uniform. Through the microphone he said, "And now for the special sunset surprise we've been promising you all evening: I give you our sister ships! Off our starboard side, behold the *Aphrodite*—born of sea foam, goddess of love, beauty, and pleasure—coming to us from her most recent stop at Cádiz. And to our port side is the *Galateia,* goddess of calm waters, joining us from Tangier. They will be sailing with us, side by side, all the way to Lisbon! Let's raise our glasses now to welcome them!"

An enormous cheer went up as the passengers leapt to their feet to snap photos of the two giant ships that had just materialized alongside the *Amphitrite.* The orchestra launched into "God Save the Queen." The British women pulled their miniature Union Jacks on sticks from their handbags. The sky filled with out-of-sync voices as the passengers on all three ships pleaded with God to protect their monarch from the knavish Scots.

While the scarlet sun plunged into the vast black waters of the Atlantic, the several thousand passengers on all three ships worked themselves up into a frenzy of patriotism with back-to-back renditions of "Land of Hope and Glory," "Jerusalem," and the inevitable "Rule, Britannia!" The sky turned midnight blue, and stars flickered on overhead, as though reflecting the hundreds of twinkling lights on the neighboring ships.

Eventually, the exhausted cowpokes fell silent and wandered off to their cabins in pursuit of the foil-wrapped Godivas their stewards had placed on their pillows.

Chapter 13

Fish Food

JESSIE WOKE UP TO THE SOUND OF A FEMALE VOICE WITH an Indian accent over the intercom, urging Mrs. Gail Savage to report immediately to the purser's desk. *What is that woman up to now?* Jessie wondered blearily as she turned over and tried to go back to sleep. But a few minutes later the same woman's voice repeated this message, sounding harried. It was time for Jessie to go run the morning clinic anyway, so she rolled out of bed and donned a fresh white shirt and knife-creased slacks from a constantly renewed supply provided by her overworked cabin steward.

Upon reaching the officers' dining room, she realized that the ship seemed to be scarcely moving. "What's going on?" she asked Stan, the lab tech, who was eating oatmeal with blueberries at one of the tables.

"Apparently a passenger has gone missing."

"Who? Mrs. Savage?"

"Yeah, I think that's her name."

"When?"

"That's what they're trying to figure out. They're reviewing the CCTV footage from last night, and they're searching the ship.

Meanwhile, the clinic is closed because the passengers have been confined to their cabins until the search is completed. So you can go back to bed."

Jessie plopped down in a chair opposite Stan. "I can't believe it. Mrs. Savage did an amazing tango on the top deck last night. Did you see it?"

Stan shook his head. "I skipped the barbecue. Don't tell Ben. I just wasn't in the mood."

"Amy trouble?" guessed Jessie.

"Yeah, I suppose she's just not that into me."

Jessie knew that it wasn't that Amy wasn't into Stan. It was, rather, that she was into Ben, with whom she flirted relentlessly in the clinic all day long. But it wouldn't help Stan to know this, so she said instead, "It's hard on a ship, isn't it? You can't get away from people. You keep bumping into them. It's like ripping the scab off a wound time after time."

"You said it."

"I'm sorry."

"Thanks, Doc."

"How did they know that Mrs. Savage was missing?"

"She was supposed to meet some guy for breakfast. When she didn't turn up, he went to her cabin, but she didn't answer the door. He had the purser page her, but she never showed up. The purser got her steward to open her door. She hadn't slept in her bed, and the chocolate from last night was still on her pillow."

"Is there anything we're supposed to be doing to help find her?"

"Not that I know of. Just staying out of the way."

"If you hear anything else, will you page me?"

"Sure thing."

Jessie grabbed a croissant and a cup of coffee and returned to her cabin. She changed into a T-shirt and sweatpants and climbed back into bed. Sipping the coffee, she opened Kat's journal and flipped to the next unread page. On it Kat had pasted a printout of an e-mail exchange with her agent, who told her that mid-list literary fiction such as she wrote wasn't selling well anymore. She suggested that Kat write a memoir. But if she insisted on writing another novel, its main character needed to be a vampire or a serial killer, preferably both.

Kat had responded that she couldn't write a memoir because she had had a happy childhood. Who wanted to read about someone who just went to school, came home, did her homework, baby-sat her siblings, set the table for supper, and then went to choir practice?

Then she had written out a recipe by Gordon Ramsay for shepherd's pie, her favorite.

Below that she had copied another Cavafy poem, this one featuring two lovers who were upset because they had to part. But Cavafy speculated that it was just as well because that way their love could remain intact and not be eroded by the passage of time.

Was Kat's interest in this poem an attempt to put a positive spin on her own death? Jesse wondered. It was a good thing she was dying, because she and Jessie would never have to face the death of their desire for each other? This sounded like a rationale that Kat, always the stoic, would cook up.

Next Kat had written several drafts of a new poem, as though in response to the Cavafy poem, with lots of words crossed out or shifted around. The final draft was titled "Swan Song II":

I know the time must come, sweetheart,
When you and I won't be attuned—
Photos in your memory book,
Borrowed shirts that weren't returned.

My finger will forget the code
I punch to dial you on the phone.
My hands won't remember how
To stroke you so you moan out loud.

But let's pretend our current bliss
Will never start to feel banal,
And let's agree to face its death
Like warriors who have dared it all.

Jessie laid the journal down on the bed. Had Kat been growing tired of her? Jessie had always regarded their love as something fixed, the Greenwich mean time of her emotional life. Had
Kat already had one foot out the door when she became ill?

This was unbearable, Jessie reflected. Why was she doing this
to herself—and to Kat? It made no sense. They had been devoted
to each other for twenty years. Why was she allowing herself to
question the integrity of their relationship? Was she mad at Kat
for leaving her? Might this be her response to Kat's having turned
away from her on her deathbed?

Jessie jumped up and again pulled on her white trousers and
shirt. Grabbing Kat's journal off the bed, she headed for the walking deck. She would find a spot from which to hurl this wretched
journal into the ocean, thereby setting herself free from the insane
doubts it was generating in her. Striding along, she spotted Major

Thapa in his whites, looking through high-powered binoculars from behind the starboard railing.

When she reached him, she called, "Good morning, Major Thapa!"

He lowered his binoculars. "Hello there, Doctor."

"Any luck?"

"It's hopeless," he admitted. "Mrs. Savage isn't anywhere on the CCTV footage, and she's nowhere to be found on this ship. We have no idea if she went overboard at all, much less when or where or why. We've turned around to retrace our route. The Portuguese coast guard is launching a helicopter and a rescue vessel, and the Spanish navy has sent up a surveillance plane to monitor their coastline. But we're just going through the motions. We don't even know where to begin to look."

"Since her husband died, she's been spending a lot of time with a gentleman host named Harry, and with a crew member named Xander, and also with a passenger named Rusty Kincaid."

"Busy lady. It was Harry who reported her missing. She was supposed to meet him for breakfast. He said he hadn't seen her since last night, in the bow after the concert. We'll have to talk with the other two."

"She seemed pretty despondent over her husband's death. I wonder if she decided to jump."

"That seems the most likely scenario. It happens a lot, you know."

"I'm sure. Can you imagine a more romantic way to end your life than to leap from a cruise ship off some foreign coast?"

"It's certainly a lot less messy for your survivors than hanging or shooting yourself. Even if you overdose, your family still has to deal with your body."

"Did Mrs. Savage leave a note?"

"No. We searched her cabin and didn't find a thing, except for her clothes and toiletries."

"What about that urn containing her husband's ashes that she's been carrying around since Alexandria?"

"No sign of that, either."

"So she and her urn have both vanished?"

"So it would seem."

Jessie kept walking until she came to the nook where the extra propellers were stored. Past them was a railing that looked directly onto the ocean. If she threw the journal over the side at that spot, it would land in the water and not on some passenger's balcony.

She studied the composition book with its mottled cover of black and white. Kat had written in it many times during her final months. If Jessie disposed of it now, she would be losing her final link to Kat. She would also forfeit her chance to figure out what Kat had been preparing to write next, as well as what she had been thinking and feeling as she had struggled to come to terms with her own death. By tossing the journal overboard, Jessie realized that she would be refusing an opportunity to learn more about this woman with whom she had shared her life for two decades. She could continue to live with her illusions, or she could face the truth, however painful. On the other hand, the journal might eventually offer some consolation.

She plopped down in a deck chair in the sun, holding tightly to the journal she had almost jettisoned. Meanwhile, in the distance she could see one of the sister ships trolling slowly back and forth, searching its assigned grid for Gail Savage. Actually, by now, they would be searching for Gail Savage's corpse. She could never have survived for this long in the chilly waters of the Atlantic. Overhead a search helicopter flapped past, while Zodiacs fanned out from the *Amphitrite* in all directions.

JESSIE WAS SITTING IN THE LOUNGE OF THE NAXOS BAR, sipping a latte while the *Amphitrite* followed a fiery pathway up the Tagus River that was reflecting the rising sun. The unsuccessful search for Gail Savage had been called off at sunset the previous evening, and the three sister ships had resumed their voyage to Lisbon. The *Amphitrite* had just passed on the port side at the river's mouth a sixteenth-century fortified tower of pale limestone, with Moorish cupolas. Now it was approaching a modern monument of concrete that featured the prow of a caravel packed with statues of the fifteenth- and sixteenth-century explorers, navigators, and missionaries who had sailed all over the globe during Portugal's famous Golden Age of Discovery.

Jessie was feeling sad about the disappearance of Gail Savage. Gail had possessed a kind of dark energy that Jessie had enjoyed. Maybe Gail was her alter ego—Morgan le Fay to her own Florence Nightingale? Gail was a woman who had done as she pleased, without regard for what other people might want from her. Of course the path between narcissism and martyrdom was a narrow one, fraught with peril. Kat used to describe a kind of Pilgrim's Progress of gender stereotypes in which men plunged off the Cliff of Narcissism, while women floundered in the Slough of Martyrdom.

This trap had ensnared Jessie's own parents. When former patients had spotted her father around town, they had practically genuflected. Meanwhile, her mother, Phi Beta Kappa and Homecoming Queen at her university, had served as a disgruntled cheerleader for him, taking her revenge via many small passive-aggressive ploys that left him miserable and searching for more Dilaudid.

But Jessie had always been drawn to women like her grandmother, who had served as a surgeon in World War I and had marched in the suffrage parades afterward—women who refused to be passive servants and victims, women who didn't shelter behind the achievements of powerful men. She had had such a mentor at Roosevelt Hospital. Dr. Isaacs had managed to look stylish even in her lab coat, with her wavy champagne-colored hair and her warm hazel eyes. She had owned stethoscopes in several different colors, and the one she wore always matched either her eyeglass frames or her nail polish.

When Jessie was looking for a job after her residency and discovered that Ben was being offered higher salaries for the same positions, she had complained to Dr. Isaacs in her office on West Fifty-ninth Street. Dr. Isaacs had replied, "Just keep your head down, Jessie, and do twice the work for twenty-five percent less money. Do most of the housework and child care at home. Deal cheerfully with men who have so many advantages they're not even aware of—but who feel threatened by your very existence. And hope that karma functions somewhere in the universe. Or else find yourself a good woman. But not me. I'm taken." Jessie had been shocked by the implication that she appeared to Dr. Isaacs to have the potential to be with a woman. But apparently mother cats could spot their own litters.

Jessie's mother had often expressed dislike of Dr. Isaacs, along with Martina Navratilova and Billie Jean King. But to have embraced her mother's version of femininity would have felt to Jessie like a death sentence. And it had, in fact, turned into one for her mother. Her father could no longer walk because of his war wounds and was addicted to painkillers. Because of his medical knowledge, each of his moles became a melanoma, and every bout of indigestion was a heart attack. Nevertheless, he insisted upon remaining at home, firing all caregivers who weren't his wife, even though she had a heart condition and was perhaps more ill than he. When Jessie tried to intervene in this sadomasochistic tarantella, her parents had joined forces to tell her to mind her own business. Her mother had died from a heart attack brought on by the exhaustion of dealing with her husband's extravagant demands and lamentations twenty-four hours a day.

But Gail Savage had perhaps overdone her determination to evade the Slough of Martyrdom. What had actually happened to her? Jessie wondered. Accident, suicide, or foul play? There was no evidence she had fallen overboard, but the entire ship had been searched, without her being found. Jessie reviewed the various areas she had toured when first boarding the *Amphitrite* in Hong Kong. She kept returning in her mind to a room that held the anchor and its chain. The giant iron anchor hung right above a shaft that opened directly onto the sea. If someone fell or jumped or was pushed down that shaft, he or she would be run over by the ship and ground to bits by the propellers. The other room that came vividly to mind contained a giant garbage compactor. Food wastes from the kitchens were pulverized in it and released into the ocean as a slurry the crew referred to as "fish food." These were grisly scenarios, but somehow or other Gail Savage had disappeared into thin air—or, more likely, into salt water.

Straight ahead of the ship was a huge suspension bridge painted the same glowing rust red as the Golden Gate Bridge. On the south side of the river just beyond it was a tall white column on which perched a statue of a man in a flowing robe— Jesus, presumably. His arms were outstretched, as though he were about to take a swan dive into the Tagus. Upriver Jessie could see some of Lisbon's famous hills, dotted with whitewashed houses sporting red-tile roofs. Atop one hill was a Moorish castle with a long crenellated wall.

Jessie returned to her analysis of Gail's death. An accident: She might have downed too much Veuve Clicquot and toppled over a railing. Suicide: She appeared genuinely despondent over her husband's death. But she certainly hadn't seemed despairing when she and Harry had performed their remarkable tango the night she vanished. In fact, although Gail and she were both recent widows, Jessie had been astonished by the pace at which Gail had been able to plunge back into the swim, while Jessie herself still hovered on the bank, paralyzed by grief.

Who on board would have wanted to harm Gail? Well, truth be told, there were several: the Australian woman who claimed Gail had stolen her gown and scorched her arm. Rodney Mullins, whose bus seat she had confiscated at El Alamein, and on whom she had toppled a Jack Daniel's after her tango. One of the men with whom she had been playing dominatrix might have recovered from his submission and turned on her to avenge his humiliation.

The ship was now creeping past Lisbon's Praça do Comércio, the Commercial Square, a vast rectangular plaza with an equestrian statue in the middle. Lining it on three sides were rows of commercial and governmental offices involved in Portugal's maritime trade. These offices, painted golden yellow, had first-floor galleries opening onto the square. On the river side, this square ran down to a wharf. For three centuries it had hosted a slave market, from which nearly six million Africans had been exported to the Americas. Like many other world-class ports, Lisbon's splendor had been founded on other people's misery.

Slowly the huge ship approached a dock at the foot of a hill, up which ran a network of twisting streets lined with the red-roofed, whitewashed houses. A crowd of official-looking men in suits and ties was waiting on the quay. Once the mooring lines had been secured, Captain Kilgore, accompanied by James Yancey, Major Thapa, and Ben, all clad in their dress uniforms, disembarked to speak with this welcoming committee. The passengers had been instructed to remain in their cabins. Many were grumbling because the stay in Lisbon was short. But the disappearance of Gail Savage clearly took precedence over their sightseeing.

The men on the quay were not happy, either. Their faces were turning red, and they were gesticulating wildly. Finally, several men in hooded white jumpsuits, who resembled a warren of earless, tailless Easter bunnies, boarded the ship.

Jessie left the lounge and walked up to the eleventh deck. Reaching Gail's suite, she discovered that the doorway was plastered with yellow crime-scene tape. Within, the people in the white jumpsuits, who had now donned blue gloves and booties and white surgical masks, were swarming the room, no doubt collecting fingerprints and DNA, just like on *CSI*.

Captain Kilgore came on the intercom and read a list of passengers and crew who were required to report to the purser's desk immediately. The other guests were free to depart on their tours.

Jessie took an elevator down to the clinic. Ben was now on duty at the front desk, but there were no patients, since most guests had left to explore Lisbon and its environs.

"So what's going on?" she asked him.

He laughed. "It turned into a regular no-man's-land out there! An FBI agent came with the American consul and an official from the State Department because Mrs. Savage was American. A Scotland Yard agent came with the British consul because the company that owns the cruise line is British. The disappearance occurred off the coast of Portugal, so the Portuguese coast guard sent a representative. We're docked in Lisbon, so the local police chief came. The *Amphitrite* is registered in the Bahamas, so a lawyer for the Bahamas Maritime Authority turned up. And the cruise line itself sent a couple of lawyers. Now they're all arguing among themselves over who has jurisdiction. Their goal is, of course, to cover their own asses if someone decides to sue."

"What's with the list of people Captain Kilgore read out?"

"They all had some kind of connection to Mrs. Savage. Various authorities are going to interview them. But it's really just a wild-goose chase."

AS NIGHT FELL, MOST OF THE CLINIC STAFF, AS WELL AS Harry and his bevy of single women guests, wound through an alley paved with black-and-white mosaics to arrive at the fado house. Its façade was faced with yellow-green-and-white tiles. Within were simple wooden tables and chairs, many already occupied by tour groups from competing cruise ships. Jessie, Ben and Mona, and Amy and Stan sat down at one table, with Harry and five wistful cougars at another. They all ordered Portuguese wines and seafood stews involving cod or sardines.

While they were eating, a woman in crimson lipstick, wearing a black dress and shawl, came out in the company of two men in suit jackets and fedoras, one carrying a twelve-string Portuguese guitar resembling a lute, and the other a regular acoustic guitar. All the diners laid down their silverware, as instructed by their waiters, so that no clattering utensils would detract from the intensity of the singing. The men began to strum and pick in a minor key.

Eventually, the woman pulled herself together and launched into one of the most mournful songs Jessie had ever heard. Although she couldn't understand the Portuguese lyrics, the melody itself conveyed a message of utter devastation. The fado songs had been composed by Portuguese sailors far from home, pining for distant loved ones.

Jessie glanced at Harry at the next table. His aging face beneath his thinning hair was sagging with grief. He had lost his love. But he wasn't supposed to have had a love while hosting on the ship. If it became known that he had romanced Gail, he would be banished from the ship. So he had been flirting listlessly all day long with the single women from the piano lounge, each of whom now believed herself to be his new favorite.

When Jessie returned her eyes to her own table, she discovered Mona gazing at her with what appeared to be longing. Jessie locked eyes with her for a long moment and felt a surge of desire. She had to admit that fado packed a punch. It was to the Portuguese what opera was to Italians, what chansons were to the French. Kat would have loved it.

As the woman's wrenching lament continued, whatever its plot may have been, the emotional pitch in the room rose, until the entire place was awash with thwarted passion. Jessie looked around at her tablemates. This was the perfect crowd for fado: Stan yearned for Amy, who yearned for Ben, who yearned for Mona, who yearned for Jessie, who yearned for Kat, who was dead. And at the neighboring table, all five women yearned for Harry, who yearned for Gail, who was also presumably dead.

By the end of the evening of these agonizing songs about the heartbreak of foiled love, everyone from the *Amphitrite* was mired in despair. They trudged in gloomy silence back down twisting alleyways of white cobblestones under a jaundice-yellow full moon, each in mourning for some unattainable beloved, like a troupe of suicidal troubadours.

Back in her cabin, Jessie discovered a new slew of downloaded e-mails from friends and family, all wanting to know where she was and when she was coming back. There were photos of grand-children in soccer uniforms and tennis outfits, as well as attach-ments of crayon drawings and report cards and term papers. It appeared she was still being regarded as a matriarch, whether she wanted to be one or not.

Chapter 14

The Valley of Death

JESSIE WAS SITTING AT LUNCH IN THE OFFICERS' DINING room with Ben, Major Thapa, and James Yancey, listening to Captain Kilgore tell about his first assignment as a captain— sailing a cargo ship full of new Toyota pickup trucks bound for Egypt southward across the Bay of Biscay.

"This bay is really deadly," he was explaining, "because the swells funneling into it from the Atlantic collide with the shallow waters atop the continental shelf. Those shallows are warm because of the Gulf Stream, so their mergence with the cold Atlantic water produces fog and violent gusts."

Jessie looked out the window beside her, where the Bay of Biscay was indeed raging. The *Amphitrite* had side stabilizers, so its lateral rolling was limited. But the bow was bucking the twenty-foot swells like a bronco with a burr beneath its saddle. Waves had been breaking over the prow all morning, and the water in the swimming pools had been sloshing across the decks. Although the purser had been handing out seasickness tablets as if to trick-or-treaters on Halloween, most passengers were in their cabins, throwing up.

Jessie had been spared this by some pressure-point wristbands Mona had brought to her cabin door early that morning. Headed for a rehearsal at the theater, she had posed in Jessie's doorway, clad in rainbow-striped workout tights, leg warmers, and a tight cropped T-shirt that left little to Jessie's imagination.

"Can you rehearse with the ship lurching around like this?" Jessie had asked.

"The songs, yes. But probably not the dance steps."

Mona held out some gray fabric wristbands. "You should try these. They really work for some people." She slipped the bands onto Jessie's wrists. As she carefully positioned the plastic nub on the pressure point of Jessie's right wrist, Jessie's arm trembled. Their eyes met.

"Gotta go," said Mona softly.

"Yes, you do." Smiling faintly, Jessie watched Mona lope down the long hallway. What the hell was that?

"A gale-force wind came up," Captain Kilgore was saying. "I panicked and cut back the power by mistake. We were supposed to be riding the waves head-on, but we got turned around so they were hitting us sideways. The waves and the gusts tipped us, until the Toyotas shifted in the hold. The ship started listing to starboard."

"Yikes!" said James Yancey. "So what did you do?"

"Luckily, we were able to fire up the engine and get turned back around, facing into the waves. Then we radioed A Coruña on the Galician coast. A tugboat came out and towed us very slowly back to their harbor. We restowed the trucks and headed toward the Strait of Gibraltar in calmer seas the next day. But I still cringe every time I think about it. It's a wonder all those new Toyotas didn't end up at the bottom of this bay, along with the thousands of ships that have gone down here over the centuries."

Jessie glanced out the window again—and spotted a pale

wave the height of the White Cliffs of Dover moving inexorably toward them. She pointed at it, but words of warning wouldn't come out of her mouth. They all turned and watched helplessly as the huge wall of water smacked the side of the *Amphitrite*, hurling plates, silverware, and wine bottles across the room. Jessie's chair skidded along the floor for several feet, and James was thrown onto the tiles.

Once the ship had steadied itself and James had regained his seat, the five just looked at one another.

Captain Kilgore said, "See what I mean? You don't mess with the Bay of Biscay. This is why the ancients put those signs on the Pillars of Hercules, warning sailors not to venture out here from the Mediterranean. The Germans called this bay 'the Valley of Death' because so many U-boats sank here."

"Any more developments around Gail Savage's disappearance?" asked Jessie.

Captain Kilgore shook his head. "Forgive me if this sounds churlish to the Americans present, but it's no surprise to us that Mrs. Savage was American. Your nation seems to export violence, with your warmongering leaders and your home arsenals of firearms."

Ben smiled sourly and replied, "Yes, but without our guns and our gift for violence, we would never have escaped from the British Empire."

Everyone laughed, and then the group broke up and headed for the door.

Out in the hallway, Ben said to Jessie, "Amy is minding the clinic this afternoon. Nobody will show up there anyhow, because they're all busy throwing up. But tomorrow it will be packed with dehydrated seniors, so go rest up."

Jessie took the elevator up to her deck and lurched along the hallway to her cabin. Once inside, she replaced her uniform with her sweatpants and T-shirt and lay down on the bed with some memos from the mailbox outside her door. Through her window she spotted the *Galateia,* also en route to Southampton, laboring through the heavy swells. Watching the sister ship pitch and heave, she realized the *Amphitrite* must be doing the same. Fortunately, she had her magic wristbands.

She wished she could just take Mona to bed and put her out of her misery. She would definitely do it once if she knew that Mona would then snap out of it—but usually if you made love to someone once, he or she expected it to continue. She did have to confess, though, to having poured gasoline on the sparks by admitting to Mona that she loved her. But it was the truth—if love meant wanting to be near Mona, wanting to hear her celestial singing voice, wanting to rest her eyes on Mona's alluring physique.

But did acknowledging love mean that two people then had to give each other orgasms and spend the rest of their lives together? Couldn't love just exist as an incorporeal enhancement to busy lives, adding a sparkle to the eye, a spring to the step, a surge of pleasure to the day, and a lift to weary spirits? But apparently courtly love wasn't permitted in the modern world. You had to put out or shut up.

She picked up a memo the cruise line had distributed to the mailboxes of all the passengers and crew concerning Gail Savage's disappearance. It included a phone number to call should any detail concerning Mrs. Savage, however trivial, occur to them after the ship's departure from Lisbon. No passengers had been detained, and the ship had been allowed to resume its posted schedule. The notice added that if additional statements were required, guests would be contacted while still on board, or once back at their home bases.

Jessie wondered if she ought to mention Rodney Mullins's bizarre interactions with Gail. He had seemed so inordinately annoyed when she had stolen his seat on the El Alamein bus, and when she had swept that drink into his lap. But surely neither of those annoyances constituted a motive for murder. And just because a man had a tattoo of a rattlesnake winding up his forearm was no reason to assume that he was homicidal. But the fact remained that it was possible an unidentified killer was roaming the ship at that very moment. It was also possible he or she might strike again. And if Jessie said nothing about what she had witnessed, she would be partially responsible. But it would be irresponsible to implicate an innocent man without any evidence. She closed her eyes and tried to figure out where her moral duty lay.

She reached over to the bedside table for the journal she had nearly flung overboard. Opening it, she flipped through the pages until she came to an as-yet-unread one on which Kat had written, "It is truly offensive that the heterosexual world is now forgiving homosexuals for being gay because we're supposedly 'born that way.' I had boyfriends and a husband, but I now choose to love a woman. Any woman in her right mind would choose the same if she looked with clear eyes at what men have done to women over the centuries. How many Jews chose to marry Nazis? It's insulting for heterosexuals to assume that if lesbians could choose, they would choose men. I can choose, and I choose a woman."

Jessie smiled. This sounded so much like Kat. She had always had a chip on her shoulder—as a southerner in the North, as a woman in a misogynistic world, as a lesbian in a homophobic world. She had gotten her training early from her Freedom Rider father, and on her commune, making the giant satirical puppets they had paraded in anti–Vietnam War demonstrations.

Later, Kat had seized every opportunity to ride buses overnight to Washington, D.C., to march for gay rights or abortion or peace, or against racism and poverty. Sometimes she had persuaded Jessie to go with her and serve as a volunteer medic. Jessie had marched proudly down Pennsylvania Avenue several times, knowing her suffragist grandmother had walked the same route. Kat had also attended many counterprotests against the right-to-lifers who were constantly trying to block access to the Burlington abortion clinic. She had always insisted that if you were a mouse being batted around by a cat, you needed to rise up on your hind legs and defy the cat—prior to the cat's final, killing swat.

Jessie was pleased to know that Kat had been aware of having chosen to be with her, just as she had chosen to be with Kat. Each of them could have led an easier life with a man, but the hassles and penalties of being labeled lesbian had evidently seemed worth it to them both. This entry made her glad she had not consigned this annoying journal to the waves.

Below this were drafts of a new poem, with the usual deletions and insertions. The finished poem was titled "Swan Song III." Certainly no one could accuse Kat of originality when it came to her titles:

> *I will soon be leaving*
> *This place where poppies bloom*
> *In rose and ocher soil*
> *By rocks from the dark side of the moon.*
>
> *I plucked wildflowers in that field*
> *That was spiked with asphodel.*

I clutched them tight while you just smiled
And said they'd wilt by night.

Of course I know that blossoms fade
And autumn storms must rage,
But I had hoped two birds in flight
Could soar above a plague.

I'll try to erase that shadowy room
By the river that drifts to the sea,
And the chasm that gaped between us
When you turned your back to me.

I'll press this poppy in my book,
And think some wishful thoughts,
And hope they help me to forget
What might have been—but is not.

So what was this about, then? If Kat had had an affair, it had apparently ended. But when had she had time for all this drama? She hadn't. She had been dying. This romance had never happened. It had been all in Kat's imagination—and now it was all in Jessie's imagination. The only back-turning that had gone on was when Kat had turned away from Jessie in the hospital.

One of Kat's most annoying traits had been her illogicality. She had flitted from topic to seemingly unrelated topic like a bee in a patch of borage. Sometimes Jessie would explain to her what she was actually trying to say. Kat would get a hunted look in her eyes and say, "Please stop telling me what I mean, Jessie. You do your life, and I'll do mine."

Jessie was so exhausted from trying to figure out her elusive lover that she turned over and went to sleep, the heaving of the ship as it struggled through the swells rocking her like a baby in a cradle.

When she awoke from her nap, the sun was low in the western sky. The ocean surface had turned as smooth as that of Lake Champlain during a placid summer dawn. She got dressed and went looking for Major Thapa, finding him in the officers' lounge, sipping an espresso. She sat down beside him in an armchair and told him about Gail Savage's having pilfered Rodney Mullins's bus seat at El Alamein and having spilled a drink on him after her tango—and about Rodney's apparent rage.

Major Thapa shrugged. "Well, thank you, Doctor, but I'm afraid facial expressions don't count as evidence."

"I understand. But the memo from the authorities said to report any detail, however trivial."

"I do appreciate it and will pass this information along. But all the competing authorities have finally agreed to label it an unexplained disappearance. Frankly, we have no clue what happened to Mrs. Savage. And unless her family makes a stink, nothing more will be done."

"Does she have a family?"

"None that we've been able to locate. No children, no living parents. Only a couple of stepchildren from whom she was estranged."

THROUGH HER OFFICE PORTHOLE JESSIE WATCHED THE steady stream of passengers disembarking from the ship to enter the arrivals terminal at the Southampton harbor. Beyond the docks were the mostly modern structures of the city, fronted by an IKEA showroom. The Luftwaffe had bombed Southampton to smithereens during World War II. Little of the ancient city had survived, apart from long stretches of the city walls. Allied soldiers had trained in the rubble for D-day, which had been launched from the ravaged docks.

She spotted Rodney Mullins in his cowboy boots and hat, walking alongside his handbag-toting wife as they left the ship. If Rodney had been involved in Gail's having vanished, he had committed the perfect crime. That morning a follow-up memo had been issued by the cruise line announcing that the investigation had been terminated. Gail's disappearance had been labeled "unexplained." If not Rodney, then anyone else in that line could have just gotten away with murder.

A ferry bound for the Isle of Wight and two cross-harbor shuttles were weaving an intricate quadrille around a huge container ship that was creeping slowly toward the mouth of the river that led to the English Channel.

She saw Harry, the priest-turned-escort, in the disembarkation line, a flight bag slung over his shoulder. During the interviews with passengers regarding Gail's disappearance, one of the singles set, disgruntled that Harry hadn't replaced Gail with herself, had reported his illicit affair with Gail. Harry had proudly acknowledged it. Mitch, the cruise director, had had no choice but to ask him to hand over his gentleman host badge and leave the ship when it docked.

Rusty Kincaid appeared on the exit gangway, his ginger hair scrambled from a sleepless night. He was so heartbroken over Gail's disappearance that he couldn't bear to stay on the ship any longer. He was catching a plane to Cincinnati from Heathrow.

It was like the conclusion of a play. All the characters with whom you had been engrossed took their curtain calls and went home to their real lives. You were left knowing that the drama that had strummed at your heartstrings had evaporated like morning dew. Jessie noted that in Kat's absence, she was the one now mixing the metaphors.

Also in the line was the Australian woman who had accused Gail of stealing her gown. She was flying home to Perth. Jessie wondered if she'd managed to retrieve her dress from Gail's cabin amid all the chaos.

Amy rushed in to inform Jessie that a maintenance man who had been hanging from ropes to paint the nose of the ship had been injured. They jogged down the central hallway and took the elevator up to the bow. When they got there, Jessie discovered Xander in his paint-splattered blue jumpsuit, lying on a wide board, groaning. He had bitten through his lower lip, and his chin was dripping blood.

She squatted down beside him. "Your back?" she asked.

He nodded, his eyes tightly shut. "I had an unbearable pain down my left leg, and now I can't feel it at all."

"We need to get you to a hospital onshore for an MRI."

"But what will I do if I can't work? I have a wife and three children in the Philippines."

"You do?" She had thought he was a freelance Lothario. Who could ever have imagined that he was a family man? "Well, I'm sure the cruise line will take care of you, Xander."

Xander chuckled bitterly. "What world are you living in, Doc?"

Jessie paged Ben, who had gone ashore with Mona to lunch with some friends of his. He soon paged her back that an ambulance would arrive on the quay. Jessie should bring the EMTs on board. The driver would know where to take Xander.

Back in the clinic after overseeing Xander's evacuation, Jessie watched through the porthole as Mona and Ben passed through the crew entry door onto the ship. Ben was wearing his whites, and Mona, a turquoise skirted suit and low heels. Mona had been a nomad in service to her talent for a long time now. But her voice wouldn't last forever, and then what would she do for a living? However, Ben, so much older, with his harem of ex-wives and children, wasn't a good bet. Mona was hitching her wagon to a falling star.

Besides, they didn't look like a couple. Or if they did, it was an unhappy one. Mona's heart definitely wasn't in it, and Ben had gone through the motions so many times now that he appeared to be on automatic pilot. Jessie would be doing them both a favor if she whisked Mona away from him. But would it be a favor to herself? Probably not. Then she would be as pathetic as Ben, snaring a younger woman so that she could pretend that she, too, was young again. Admittedly, the chemistry was there. She couldn't deny the tremor that had shaken her arm when Mona had stroked her wrist in the Bay of Biscay, or the pang of desire that had passed between them in the Lisbon fado house. But there were limits to chemistry. And since she was experienced enough to know what those were, she was clearly the one tasked with riding the brakes.

Chapter 15

Metaphors

AS THE *AMPHITRITE* ROUNDED THE ISLE OF WIGHT AND headed toward the English Channel, Jessie sat in the main dining room with Mrs. P., eating a full English breakfast of eggs, sausages, tomatoes, and cold toast with marmalade.

The atmosphere on board had shifted noticeably that morning as they cast off from the Southampton wharf. What had seemed an interminable journey to Jessie back in the Arabian Sea had now ended for well over half the passengers who had witnessed the foiled pirate attack in the Red Sea and the refugee rescue in the Mediterranean. Those people had disembarked the previous day, taking their grief, guilt, indifference, or irritation home with them. The new passengers were mostly Americans who didn't like to fly, or who wanted to avoid jet lag. They were heading to New York after business or pleasure in London or on the Continent, anointing the weary, battered ship with their brash optimism. Or they were Brits bound for New York's outlet malls with empty suitcases, also full of good cheer because of the bargains they expected to snag.

"It feels so strange having all those people we traveled with throughout Southeast Asia and the Middle East gone now. It's almost as though it were all a dream," she observed to Mrs. P.

"You get used to that. People and their dramas come and go on board, just like on dry land, only faster."

"But the whole mood has shifted, with all these smiling Americans with good dental work."

"Yes, in spite of the stereotypes about charming English people, it turns out many Americans are actually more polite. They let you go ahead of them into elevators. And if the elevator is full, they wait for the next one, instead of cramming themselves in behind you. It's fascinating watching the changes as the various nationalities get on and off. For instance, sometimes Chinese passengers wear surgical masks around the ship. To fend off our wicked Western germs, I guess. But is there any chance you might join us full-time here on the *Amphitrite*?"

Jessie smiled. "It's definitely an option, and a very appealing one."

Just then, Mrs. P. started gasping for air. She grabbed her throat as her face turned purple.

"Are you choking?" Jessie felt herself becoming calm and detached as she transitioned into crisis mode.

Mrs. P. nodded frantically.

Jessie stood up and pulled back Mrs. P.'s chair. "I'm going to do the Heimlich on you. You'll be fine."

Jessie lifted her to her feet and stood behind her with a fist positioned over her solar plexus. She jerked upward several times. A chunk of sausage came flying from Mrs. P.'s mouth onto the carpet. Mrs. P. fell back into her chair and took a gulp of water.

"Thank you," she whispered.

"Let me help you back to your room."

Mrs. P. got to her feet and walked shakily across the dining room with Jessie holding her arm. The entire restaurant erupted into cheers and applause. Jessie smiled and nodded. She wondered if Mrs. P. realized that the good Lord might have intended for her to choke to death on that sausage she had so greedily inhaled. She would have died if another mortal had not intervened with an artificial medical technique. Yet she expected young women who were unintentionally pregnant to pay for their mistakes their whole lives long.

After leaving Mrs. P. at her room, Jessie went out on the walking deck to watch the ship sail along the Cornish coast toward the open ocean. Emerald green fields topped the rocky cliffs that plunged right down into the waves. This was the same route followed by both the *Mayflower* and the *Titanic,* with their drastically different fates.

In a few days the ship would dock in Brooklyn. Mona would disembark there. Ben would proceed to the Caribbean, South America, and the South Pacific. Would Ben and Mona's romance, or whatever it was, continue?

As for herself, she faced some decisions. She concluded she needed to do a rule-out of her options, as though diagnosing a patient. She sat down in a lounge chair and took a small notebook and pen from her knapsack. She wrote: "(1) Continue on the *Amphitrite* as a physician. (2) Continue on the ship as a permanent passenger. (3) Stay in New York. (4) Stay in New York with Mona. (5) Return to the Burlington ER. (6) Return to Burl. and retire. (7) Join Doctors Without Borders. (8) Enroll in a retirement community and play golf."

Studying her list, she crossed out number eight. She wasn't yet ready for golf. Beyond that, she couldn't say. She flipped her notebook shut and returned it to her knapsack.

Burlington was a wonderful place, but most people she knew there were coupled. It could be lonely, especially in the winter, when everyone cocooned with loved ones to eat popcorn and binge-watch TV series on Netflix. At least in New York City you could go out at any hour of the day or night and be surrounded by other lonely people.

She smiled sardonically, recalling the last line of the Cavafy poem she had memorized for Kat's service, about the ultimate goal of the journey to Ithaca:

> *As wise as you will have become, with so much experience,*
> *you will understand, by then, these Ithacas; what they*
> *mean.*

Well, she was damned if she understood what Ithaca meant. Based on what little she'd grasped about poetry under Kat's tutelage, she supposed Ithaca represented home, the home Odysseus wanted to return to if he could escape from Calypso's love cave, the home where his wife, Penelope, was waiting for him. Kat and she had had a home. But Kat was no longer waiting there for her return, so that home was no longer a home. She had to make a new home for herself, one not haunted by Kat's absence from it. This journey was supposed to have reconciled her to Kat's absence, but instead she was more bereft now than when she had first boarded, in a state of such mind-numbing denial. The possible implications of the three "Swan Song" poems had upset her, maybe even more deeply than she had yet acknowledged. She decided to confide in Kat's best friend, Louise.

Returning to her cabin, she got out Kat's journal and typed up the three poems titled "Swan Song." Then she sent a chatty e-mail to Louise, telling her a bit about the voyage but not responding to the question in Louise's last e-mail about when she was returning to Burlington. She concluded by telling Louise, "I found some poems in Kat's final journal. Although I've tried to understand them, I have a tin ear for poetry, as you well know. Would you be willing to answer some questions I have about them?"

Louise told her by return e-mail to send the poems along, that she'd be pleased to read them and tell Jessie what she thought, but that she had to teach a class in a few minutes. Also, she wanted to take her time with the new poems, so she'd be back in touch in a day or two.

JESSIE LOOKED OUT THE FRONT WINDOW OF THE NAXOS Bar at the surging black sea. The walking deck had been closed all day due to high winds off the North Atlantic. Even on the couple of days when the deck had been open, Jessie had had to wear her parka and balaclava, brought from Vermont. The few people out walking had moved quickly, hunched over against the cold. It was quite a shock after the blistering sun in Southeast Asia and the Middle East. No wonder the Islamic invaders of Europe had felt such contempt for the barbarians of the north, who wore smelly animal furs and huddled in their hovels for warmth.

"This is the same route, in reverse, that my father took on the lead ship of a troop convoy during World War Two," Jessie told Ben, who had invited her for a drink. "He did an appendectomy, using dinner forks as retractors, while his ship sent down depth charges to destroy the German subs beneath them."

Ben whistled. "They really were the Greatest Generation, weren't they? He was an impressive man, your father."

"I forgot that you met him."

"Yeah, he came to Roosevelt once to visit you. He was a huge man in every respect!"

"Yes, he was a war hero, and he paid for it for the rest of his life. His legs were shattered by a German machine gun, and he eventually became unable to walk even with braces and crutches. After you met him, he got addicted to painkillers. Not long before he died, I realized that he had undiagnosed PTSD."

"How did you figure that out?"

"I was with him when he had a flashback. We were watching a war movie, and he freaked out and insisted that I race into the corridor of his nursing home to get us some helmets and flak jackets."

"Yes, it can last a lifetime if it isn't treated—and sometimes even when it is treated."

"Fine physicians my brothers and I were, huh, not to have even noticed his suffering?"

"I don't imagine he made it easy for anyone to help him."

Jessie shook her head. "No one except my mother. He wore her out with his demands for help."

"Well, the reason I asked you here tonight is because I wanted to thank you for doing such a fantastic job on short notice these past six weeks. And I wanted to invite you to renew your contract. You're very skilled and very conscientious, and we'd be thrilled if you'd continue with us to Sydney. On a personal note, I've enjoyed having you on board. We work well together, and I have complete confidence in your abilities."

"Thank you, Ben. I've enjoyed it, too. Your offer is tempting, but I'm not sure what I want to do next. Can I give you an answer in the morning?"

"I had hoped you'd say yes right away. But tomorrow morning will be fine. I'll keep my fingers crossed."

Back at her cabin, Jessie discovered an e-mail from Louise, saying that she'd read "Swan Song": "Its lyricism is almost old-fashioned. I guess Kat reverted to her southern roots at the end of her life. Thank you for letting me read it. I was quite moved. What questions do you have? I don't want to put words into Kat's mouth, but I'll do my best to answer them."

Jessie took a deep breath and then asked Louise if it was possible that Kat had been in love with someone else when she wrote the "Swan Song" poems.

Louise answered immediately: "No, Jess. After she met you, that was it for her. The three parts of 'Swan Song' comprise one poem, and it isn't about you and her, or about her and anybody else. It's a composite of all her loves—and of her love of life, most of all. More than that, it's her confrontation with her own death. In mythology, a swan is supposedly silent its entire life, but then it sings an eerily beautiful melody as it lies dying. You know how Kat loved music, and this is her final song. Let me know if you have other questions, but please never doubt the love that you and Kat shared."

Jessie lay back on her pillows and pondered this answer. She felt tears begin to well up. She hadn't cried in years, but here on the *Amphitrite* she'd been crying every other week. However, she didn't want Mona to come comfort her again. So she sat up and dried her eyes with her sheet. But how was she to know if Louise was telling the truth? Louise was Kat's best friend. If Kat had had a new love, Louise wouldn't tell Jessie, out of loyalty to Kat, and from not wanting to hurt Jessie. What if Louise herself had been the new love?

Jessie hurled Kat's journal across the room. It hit the wall and slid down it to the floor. As she looked at the crumpled heap in the corner, she had to confess that she had definitely lost her fabled capacity for detachment.

After struggling for some time to calm herself, Jessie realized that her therapist of long ago would have pointed out that she had been projecting. Every fiber of Jessie's body knew that there had been no one else for Kat. Jessie had made the whole thing up because Kat's having been unfaithful to her would have made it easier to let her go. But the reality was that Jessie had been toying with the idea of getting involved with Mona. Jessie was the one who had had her eye on someone else, not Kat.

The intercom clicked overhead. Captain Kilgore's voice came on: "Just to let you know that we're now passing over the spot where the *Titanic* struck an iceberg that fateful night in April of 1912, just a little over one hundred years ago. The remains of the *Titanic* now lie below us on the ocean floor. But hey, no worries, folks, I'm in charge now!"

Jessie felt a twinge of panic remembering his nearly sinking the cargo ship in the Bay of Biscay. He was the age of her son, Anthony, and he used language like "No worries." This was not reassuring. But she had other topics to fret about, so she took a melatonin and turned out her light.

WHEN JESSIE AWOKE, A PALE NORTHERN SUN WAS PEEKING out from behind some storm clouds the color of fresh bruises. She reached over to her bedside table for her post-cruise options list. She had apparently reached some decisions during melatonin-fueled dreams that she couldn't recall. She crossed off numbers one and two. She had had enough of the *Amphitrite.* It had originally seemed like a floating palace. But her cabin now felt as confining as one of the dog kennels on the top deck. It was a luxurious kennel, true, but it had become claustrophobic.

She also crossed out option number five. Medicine no longer appealed to her now that insurance companies were telling doctors how much time to spend with patients—when every decent doctor knew that healing involved time and attention at least as much as it did tests and medications. Her father had quit medicine when faced with having to learn laparoscopic techniques. She was quitting because she knew she couldn't help anyone in the fifteen minutes insurance companies were now allotting doctors. In addition, although her professional detachment had been failing her recently, she wasn't sure she missed it. Her raw emotions weren't always pleasant to experience, but they did make her feel like a full-fledged member of the human race.

Then she crossed out number seven. All her working life she had tried to alleviate the suffering of others. It was time now to crawl out of the Slough of Martyrdom and confront her own suffering. She had apparently figured out in her sleep that her chronic grief aboard this ship wasn't entirely about Kat or her parents, or even about that battered Sudanese girl. To accept their deaths meant accepting her own death. Letting go of Kat's body meant facing the necessity of eventually letting go of her own body.

She had had many billets-doux from Death lately—varicose veins, knee pain when she jogged, sun damage on her face, extra pounds around her middle, acid reflux when she drank too much alcohol. Little Post-it notes to warn her that her body was like an old jalopy, with fraying tubes and hoses and clogged filters—notes to remind her that one day she, too, would face a blind date with Death.

How much longer did she have—a day, a month, a year, ten

years, twenty years? If you could only know, you could plan your indulgences so that the check your children wrote to pay for your cremation would bounce. As it was, you had to plan to die tonight, and also plan to live to one hundred, both at the same time. Either way, you needed to be ready—if that was possible. She had spent her career helping her patients stay alive. Now she had to help herself learn how to die.

But death might be like childbirth. While pregnant with Anthony, she had taken a course in Lamaze techniques for a drug-free delivery. But once she was actually in labor, she had begged for every drug on the pharmacy shelves.

The only options now left on her list were New York, Burlington, or Mona.

She got up and went to the officers' lounge. Ben was breakfasting alone. She thanked him for the job offer but declined. "I have to go back to Vermont and deal with some stuff," she heard herself telling him.

"I'm sorry, Jess, but if you change your mind, please let me know."

Jessie nodded. She noted, as she grabbed a coffee and headed out the door to the clinic, that Mona was sitting alone on the far side of the lounge.

When Jessie arrived at the clinic, she supplied a few passengers with medications they had forgotten to pack. Then she went into her office and sat down at her desk. Business was slow on this transatlantic crossing because passengers with issues had seen their own physicians before they left, or would see them once they landed in New York.

Jessie had brought along Kat's journal. She read the three parts of "Swan Song" as one poem, as Louise had recommended. For the first time, she saw that part one was about the melodrama of young love. Part two was about the comfortable tedium of middle-aged love. And part three was about the loss of love—and of life. Jessie had been deeply narcissistic to believe that it was all about her. Kat had been dealing with something far more urgent.

Just then, Mona appeared in the doorway in torn jeans and her Broadway Cares T-shirt. "Hey," she said softly.

"Hey."

When Mona said nothing further, Jessie asked, "Is there something I can do for you?" As though she didn't know.

"I just wanted to know where you're going once we land in Brooklyn."

"I'm not sure yet." She still had three options, and Mona was one of those. Kat would have added a fourth: the unknown.

"If you're at loose ends, you're welcome to stay at my apartment. I don't have another gig for three weeks. We could explore the five boroughs together."

"That's an interesting idea. Can I get back to you?" She had never before been propositioned with a tour of the five boroughs as a lure.

"Sure. The offer holds good all the way to the wharves of Brooklyn."

"Where's Ben going while the ship is docked in Brooklyn?"

"No idea. Probably visiting one of his squadron of ex-wives. I told you he was just a distraction. Luckily, it seems I was one for him, too."

Jessie nodded.

"I just have one question," said Mona in an unsteady voice.

"What's that?"

"Why did you tell me on Malta that you love me?"

Jessie frowned. Her chickens were coming home to roost. "Because I do."

"What do you mean by that?"

"Well, I mean that I admire you—your beautiful voice, your courage in pursuing your vocation. I mean that I enjoy talking with you. That I find you intelligent and funny. That I like your looks." Jessie paused.

"That's it?"

"Isn't that enough?"

"You know that it could mean a lot more than that."

"It could for someone who wasn't in mourning."

"What is this—the nineteenth century or something?"

"Those Victorians understood some things about human psychology that those of us living in the age of instant gratification have lost sight of."

"I've always found that the best way to get over one person is to turn to someone new."

Jessie bit her tongue to prevent herself from saying that Mona had never been with someone for twenty years, so she didn't know what she was talking about. Many songs Mona sang concerned love, but Jessie had her doubts about whether Mona had ever really experienced it—and she still didn't know if she wanted to be her coach.

"I love you, too," ventured Mona. "But for me that means that I want to know you in every way possible."

Jessie sighed. "So you mind that we haven't made love?"

"I just don't understand what it is that you want from me."

"I'm happy with what we've got."

Mona shook her head in disbelief. "Well, let me know if you want to come stay with me and discuss this further."

"Okay, I will. Thanks."

Mona waved and then turned around and left.

Jessie heaved another sigh. God, it was so tempting just to

anesthetize herself with lust and get lost in the delirium of exploring a new body and an unfamiliar psyche.

Shaking her head at her hopeless self, she returned to Kat's journal and discovered this quote: "I vowed to love him in the right way, to love even his love for another. Admittedly, I never thought I would have to face this so soon." Jessie recognized these lines. A few months before Kat's death, they had gone to the Plaza 9 movie theater in Burlington to watch the Met's live transmission of *Der Rosenkavalier,* Kat's favorite opera. The line in question had been sung by Renée Fleming, playing an aristocratic woman who was trying to accept the fact that her younger lover was falling in love with a woman his own age. As Renée sang these lines, Kat had reached over in the darkened theater and taken Jessie's hand in her own and squeezed it tightly.

It amused Jessie to think that Kat had been identifying with Fleming's role, because in her prime she would have identified with the androgynous alto playing the frisky young man, as opposed to the wise and generous older woman. Kat would have hated the idea that she herself had become wise and generous as she faced her own death. But she had. Jessie thought about Kat's final words to her: "Don't mourn for me too long, Jess. Find someone new and be happy again."

Kat had accepted the fact that Jessie would move on. She had wanted that for her. And who was Jessie to disobey the wishes of a dying woman?

Once her shift ended, Jessie returned to the eleventh deck. Pausing at her own door, she turned and walked slowly over to Mona's door. She would do as Kat had instructed. She would accept Mona's invitation and see where it might lead. She could always call it off if it turned out to be a bad idea. She paused for a long time with her fist raised. Finally, she knocked. Mona didn't answer. She knocked again. Still no answer. Mona was probably rehearsing at the theater.

Jessie returned to her own door and unlocked it. As she entered her cabin, she spotted a figure at the far end of the corridor. Even at such a distance Jessie could tell that it was Mona. But she looked so much like Kat at the same age that it was uncanny—tall and shapely, with a mop of naturally curly auburn hair. Not only did they own identical emerald collars; they both loved almost every style of music. The only difference was that Mona could carry a tune.

Jessie shut her door and leaned back against it, heaving a sigh of relief that Mona had been out when she had knocked. If she went home with Mona, she would crawl ashore in a few months, after their tsunami of hormones had receded, and find Death still waiting for her, patiently pasting yellow Post-it notes all over her aging flesh. She had to negotiate a truce with this enemy combatant before she could even consider touring the five boroughs with Mona.

Mona would never be able to understand this. The young and the aging lived in parallel universes that never intersected. The young hadn't yet experienced the slow torture of losing friends and family members, one after another, some in great pain, until your own heart felt as hollowed out as a Halloween pumpkin. Sadly, she now saw that it wasn't that she was too old for Mona. It was, rather, that Mona was too young for her. This confrontation with the reality of mortality was something Jessie had to face—and had to face alone.

Jessie ordered a hamburger, fries, and a Michelob from room service and changed into her happy-face pajamas. Then she climbed into bed with Kat's journal. The next page read: "Sexuality, creativity, and spiritual experience are all different manifestations of the same energy. Metaphors work only because matter already possesses an underlying unity that allows you to compare one fragment of it to another. E=mc2. Energy is speeded-up matter. Matter is slowed-down energy. Is it possible to identify with that energy itself, without needing to manifest it as matter? Is it possible to *become* that energy?"

Next she had written out a story called "The Tale of the Sands." She had spent an exchange year in London in college, during which she had met some Afghans who had introduced her to their tradition of teaching stories. She had read books of these stories ever since, but she rarely talked about them. Once she gave a collection to Jessie. Jessie had read a couple, but they hadn't meant anything to her. Besides, when she had time to read, she needed to catch up on *JAMA* articles.

"The Tale of the Sands" concerned a stream that was trying to reach the sea. It arrived at a desert and could go no farther without drying up. The sands of the desert advised the stream to rise up as a mist and allow the wind to carry it across the wasteland. The stream did this. On the far side of the desert, the mist turned back into water and fell into the ocean as drops of rain.

There was a knock at her door. For a moment Jessie wondered if it was Mona and if she should pretend not to be there. It seemed there were definite limits to her willpower. But when she finally opened the door, a waiter carried in a tray containing her burger. He set it down on her desk and departed.

As she munched her fries and sipped her beer, Jessie understood what she had to do: She had to go back to Burlington, get her and Kat's pontoon boat out of storage, and float around Lake Champlain with a thermos of coffee, a sandwich, and some sunscreen. She had to watch the final patches of April snow on the peaks of the Adirondacks as they melted into rivulets that cascaded off the rocky cliffs into a lake that had so recently been ice. She had to watch the warm spring air creep across the frigid water until steam rose up, steam that would thicken into fog, fog that would burn off in the heat of the noonday sun. She had to watch the vapor suspended in the towering wine-dark thunderheads as it condensed into raindrops, raindrops that would crystallize into hail, hail that would pelt back down into the waiting water. She had truly to accept the fact that, as Kat had written about the archaeological torte that was Alexandria, the only constant in life is change.

LOOKING OUT HER CABIN WINDOW THE NEXT AFTERNOON, Jessie spotted the Statue of Liberty, lichen green on her pedestal of gray concrete. She felt a surge of pleasure to be back in her terrible and magnificent homeland.

As the ship docked, she exited from her cabin for the last time. Mona was coming out her own door.

"Mona!" she called.

Mona turned and looked at her with a blank expression. She was upset. Jessie couldn't help it. She couldn't help *her.* She couldn't help anyone else anymore. She had to help herself first, the way stewardesses warned airplane passengers to put on their own oxygen masks before attempting to assist their seatmates.

"I'm sorry I didn't get back to you. I'm afraid I can't visit you right now. I've got some things I need to take care of in Burlington."

Mona nodded, clearly disappointed and a little annoyed. And Jessie had to admit that she had led her on.

Jessie opened her arms. Reluctantly, Mona moved into them. They hugged for a long time. Jessie had to marshal the full force of her self-restraint in order to lower her arms and step back. But she needed to face the future, rather than trying to re-create the past, with Mona standing in as a body double for Kat.

"Let's keep in touch?" suggested Jessie.

"Whatever," muttered Mona as she turned away. "No worries, Jessie. It's all good."

Jessie let her leave and watched her go, pulling her battered blue suitcase down the long carpeted corridor. Jessie would collect her own bags in the arrivals hall, take an Uber to La Guardia, and hop a plane to Burlington.

THE PONTOON BOAT, DRIVEN BY ANTHONY, HEADED TOWARD the middle of Lake Champlain. Martin, Malcolm, and Cady sat on the green vinyl benches with Kat's and Jessie's six grandchildren, ages four to fifteen. The children's spouses, as well as Kat's and Jessie's friends and siblings, ex-husbands and ex-girlfriends and their current partners, had volunteered to stay at the condo and drink, since there wasn't enough room on the boat for everyone. Martin's restaurant was catering a feast there once the boaters returned.

Louise sat up front beside Jessie, the ebony jewelry box containing Kat's ashes in her lap. It was a sunny May afternoon with a mother-of-pearl sky overhead. But the breeze was chilly, so everyone was wearing jeans, fleece or down jackets or vests, and running shoes or hiking boots. Malcolm had managed to access Kat's playlist on her iPhone and hook it up to a tiny speaker that was now broadcasting an eclectic array of songs. At the moment, Otis Redding was singing "I've Been Loving You Too Long (To Stop Now)."

Anthony cut the engine, and the pontoon boat drifted slowly to a halt as ripples lapped its battered metal sides. At this spot, the lake was completely surrounded by mountains, the blue-gray Adirondacks on the New York side and the darker Green Mountains in Vermont.

Malcolm clicked off the music, and Jessie stood up. "Thank you for coming with me today to say our final farewell to Kat. I'm sure you all know how much she loved you, because she was never shy about telling us so. And I know you all miss her as much as I do. But she wanted us to be happy remembering the fun we had with her while she was here, rather than being sad that she's no longer with us."

She nodded to Malcolm, and he switched on Renée Fleming singing the "Recordare" from Verdi's *Requiem.* Jessie took the ebony box from Louise and removed the plastic bag containing Kat's ashes. She leaned out over the railing and slowly broadcast the pale gray remains of Kat's body across the shimmering water.

Then Cady gave a burgundy peony, Kat's favorite flower, to every grandchild. Each came forward and tossed his or her flower into the water and recounted a favorite memory of Kat. One remembered flying kites out over the lake with her. Another recalled Kat's tossing bread crumbs onto the beach and calling down flocks of screeching seagulls. They talked of Kat's having taught them to swim and water-ski and fish, to drive motorboats and Jet Skis, to paddle canoes and kayaks. They laughed about her strumming her baritone uke and singing "Froggy Went A-Courtin'" to them as toddlers, with special voices for the various animals.

After the grandchildren had finished, Jessie stood up again and said, "Kat kept a journal for each of her books. At the end of her final one she wrote down what she wanted me to tell you: She was very proud of all of you, and she asked me to remind you that since you have had so many advantages—enough food, warm clothing, nice houses, good schools, parents and grandparents who love you—you have an obligation to defend those who don't have these things."

The children and grandchildren nodded impatiently, having heard this exhortation from Kat all their lives.

"She also asked me to read you a quote. It's from Julian of Norwich, a woman who was a religious hermit. She lived in fourteenth-century England. The fourteenth century was a terrible time. A famine and a plague killed half the people in England. Also, a war with France raged on for a hundred years. But here are the words that Julian heard in a mystical vision concerning this horror: 'And all shall be well, and all shall be well, and all manner of thing shall be well.'

"Kat wanted you to know that no matter how difficult your lives may become, everything will be okay in the end. Your job is to be brave and always to fight for what you know is right."

Jessie studied her and Kat's grandchildren, some resembling Kat, others herself. Their hearts were full of so many unrealistic hopes and dreams. Whatever else life might hold in store for her, it was her responsibility to ease their paths through this darkening world. They were the future—if this tortured planet were to have a future.

The boat had drifted away from the patch of cloudy water where Kat's ashes were now dissolving, studded with the sodden burgundy peonies, like clots of fresh blood. A school of perch rose up from the deep to snap at the tiny shards of white bone still floating there.

Jessie watched some seagulls sweep out from the Vermont

shoreline. They circled overhead with raucous shrieks. One gull plummeted down from the sky to seize an unwary perch in its beak. The gull hurried away, wings beating madly, protecting its plunder from pursuers, the scales of the dying perch flashing silver in the sun.

ACKNOWLEDGMENTS

Heartfelt thanks to these friends, without whose advice and encouragement this book wouldn't exist: Ina Danko, Stephanie Dowrick, Vicky Wilson, Jane Shaw, Robert Gottlieb, Carol Edwards, and Marc Jaffee.

A NOTE ON THE TYPE

The text of this book was set in Garamond No. 3. It is not a true copy of any of the designs of Claude Garamond (ca. 1480–1561), but an adaptation that probably owes as much to the designs of Jean Jannon, a Protestant printer in Sedan in the early seventeenth century, who had worked with Garamond's romans earlier in Paris. This particular version is based on an adaptation by Morris Fuller Benton.

Typeset by Scribe,
Philadephia, Pennsylvania

Printed and bound by Berryville Graphics,
Berryville, Virginia

Designed by Betty Lew